GUNSMOKE RECKONING

Gallom's gun came into sight and roared. Sam Chord jerked as lead struck him. He reeled back a couple of paces and fell to the ground, his gun still in his holster. The crowd's combined voice rose in an angry snarl and the deputies hefted their shotguns for they knew it would be fight or end up doing a cottonwood hoe down. Gallom had gone way too far when he shot down the old man in cold blood.

'Lousy murdering skunk, Gallom,' said Chord's old partner in a rage and grief filled voice. 'I'll see you hang for this.'

'Yeah?' snarled Gallom, fear, hate and menace mingling in his tones. 'You'll have to take me first.'

'*I can do that, too*!'

The voice came from the corner of the saloon and it brought every eye, including Gallom's, to the speaker and caused the crowd to back off out of range of bullets which all knew would soon be flying.

Standing at the corner, his *amigos* in a loose half-circle behind him, was Dusty Fog.

Books by J. T. EDSON
Arranged in chronological order of stories

† In preparation   * Awaiting publication
and published by CORGI BOOKS

THE RIO HONDO WAR

CORGI BOOKS

A DIVISION OF TRANSWORLD PUBLISHERS LTD

A NATIONAL GENERAL COMPANY

THE RIO HONDO WAR
A CORGI BOOK 552 09347 5

Originally published in Great Britain
by Sabre Books

PRINTING HISTORY
Sabre edition published 1964
Second edition published 1966
Third edition published 1967
Corgi edition published 1970
Corgi edition reissued 1973

This book is set in Times 10 pt.

Corgi Books are published by Transworld Publishers, Ltd.,
Cavendish House, 57–59 Uxbridge Road, Ealing, London W.5.

Made and printed in Great Britain by
Richard Clay (The Chaucer Press), Ltd., Bungay, Suffolk

The Rio Hondo War

CHAPTER ONE

I NEED A MAN

'You're loco, Boss!'

The words came in a startled croak from the tall tanned man's lips as he stood behind Basil Drinkwater and stared at the pointer's tip as it touched the map of Texas set up on an easel.

'Why's that, Bill?' asked Drinkwater, studying the man.

'That's the Rio Hondo country,' Bill Acre replied as if he need say no more.

'I'm aware of that. It's ideal for our purposes. One of the more easterly and better civilised cattle counties. Just over the county line here, at back of the town of Diggers Wells, I have bought the ranch which is being used as a holiday resort for rich easterners who want the thrills if not the rigours of western life. We've our own men there, and in Diggers Wells we even have our own town marshal. I can move into the ranch as a visitor and command things without anybody knowing my interests in the business.'

For a long moment Acre studied his boss without speaking.

Somehow the big man did not seem to fit into the atmosphere of rich, well-organised elegance of the room in which he found himself. He stood bareheaded, his black Stetson hat resting on a table by the door. The face had a leathery tan which certainly did not find its origin anywhere in the great city of New York which sprawled out beyond the walls of Drinkwater's town house. He wore a leather coat of range style and, from the way it was fastened, the string tie around his neck was not a usual item of dress in his life. Nor were his high-heeled boots, showing from under the levis trousers, suited to city life and wear. In everything Bill Acre gave off an aura of the range country, the vast, untrammelled and untamed west beyond the Mississippi River.

'It's just not worth the trying, Boss,' he finally said.

A smile played on Drinkwater's lips at the repeated use of the respectful 'Boss' from a man so much taller, stronger and more able in practical matters than he himself would ever be. It gave him, a small man, a sense of power and Basil Drinkwater was painfully aware of his lack of inches. In height he stood on more than five foot six and had a slim build which the elegant fashions of New York tended to emphasise rather than hide. He wore his clothes well for all that and he was handsome enough even without the added attraction of being known as a rich and powerful man in the business world of the United States' largest city.

'You really believe it, don't you, Bill?' he asked, fingers playing with his watch chain as he spoke.

'I know it, Boss,' replied Acre, holding out his big left hand so he could tick off points on the fingers. 'First off there's Hondo Fog, he's county sheriff, town marshal and about every other damned thing, and hell on wheels where law enforcement's concerned. Mannen Blaze's the local judge and a ringy old goat who can still handle a ten gauge scatter when there's need for it, which same there isn't much in the Rio Hondo County. They've kept the county free of crime for years between them. Then there's the Blaze boys out at the Double B. Buck and Pete are bad enough but young Red's a terror, and they've seven men who would rather fight than eat. The O.D. Connected runs seventeen hands full time, counting Ole Devil's floating outfit. All ringy cusses who can handle their end in any man's fight. Then happen Ole Devil opens his mouth and hollers he'll have nigh on half of Texas guarding his front porch and the rest riding circle around the house. Wes Hardin's his nephew, you've heard tell of him?'

'He's a criminal, isn't he?' Drinkwater replied. 'A murderer.'

'He's wanted for killing, but he's no criminal. Shot down a nigger as was set to use a razor on him. That was right after the war and there wasn't no crime so bad thought of by the Yankees as killing a nigger, no matter what that same nigger aimed to do to a man.'

'They seem to have you scared, Bill,' said Drinkwater, looking at the other man in frank curiosity.

8

Certainly Acre had proved his courage when Drinkwater first began to work on his scheme for a vast cattle empire in the Texas range country. He led the men who successfully drove off the owners of two ranches up Uvalde way and perfected a technique which worked very well. Until this evening Drinkwater had never seen the burly westerner show any sign of fear, or worry about starting to take over a new area.

'Sure they've got me scared, Boss,' Acre stated flatly. 'Those other places we took were like babes in arms compared with the O.D. Connected, even without counting Ole Devil's floating outfit.'

'And who, or what, might Ole Devil's floating outfit be?'

Acre, a man not given to freely showing emotions, looked surprised that a man so knowing in most matters should have failed to hear of Ole Devil's floating outfit.

'It's who, not what, Boss,' he explained. 'It's four hell-twisters Ole Devil lets handle any trouble that comes his way, or to his friends. There's Mark Counter, and he's stronger than any three men you can name. One of the best rough-house brawlers in the west when he's pushed into it. Only he's not just brawn, he's smart and he's real fast with his guns. Then there's the Ysabel Kid. They don't come no tougher, nor meaner in a fight, than the Kid. He's part Comanche, claims to be the kin to ole Chief Long Walker and I wouldn't want to be the man who called him a liar. The Kid's real good with that ole Dragoon Colt he totes, and don't you let nobody tell you no man's good with the old Dragoon. The Kid is, but he's better with his bowie knife and there's few who can touch him with a rifle. Down on the Rio Grande they say that when you see the Kid make a hit with his rifle it's plumb ordinary, but happen you see him miss his mark, you done seen a miracle, and I'm not doubting them any. The Kid's bad medicine. He can move through thick brush quieter'n a buck Apache and follow sign like no other man I know. The other one's a boy called Waco. It's his only name, but he handles his guns like to beat most folks with a whole flow of words to their names. One time he rode for Clay Allison, did Waco, and the man, or boy, don't live who rode for Allison without being a regular snake with his guns. That boy alone, he'd take some moving happen he dug his heels in.'

9

'You only mentioned three names, doesn't the other matter among all that torrent of talent?'

'That depends, Boss,' replied Acre dryly. 'He was a Confederate Army captain at seventeen, one of the best cavalry leaders in the war, on either side. Since then he's been Ole Devil's segundo at the O.D. Connected, a trail boss with the best of them. He was the man who tamed Quiet Town* when she rode wild and woolly just after the war. Comes to a point he's just about the fastest man alive.'

Acre paused as if he thought he'd said all that need be said and Drinkwater must know who he meant.

'And who might this wonder-man be?' asked Drinkwater, with the lofty disdain of a big city man dealing with a country dweller.

'You mean you've never heard tell of Dusty Fog?'

The smile left Drinkwater's face. He looked at Acre, trying to decide if the big man was joking. Yet never had Acre appeared more serious. Drinkwater stopped toying with his watch chain. Of course he had heard of Dusty Fog, ex-Captain of the Texas Light Cavalry and, as Acre said, one of the most outstanding cavalry officers produced by the Civil War.

'I've heard of him.'

'I tell you, Boss. I'll stack up against ordinary cowhands or hired guns. But I'm sure not locking horns with Cap'n Fog and his *amigos*. And, happen you've got the good sense I credit you with, you'll steer clear of them too, Boss. I can name you maybe a dozen places we could get in Texas with nowheres near the trouble we'll get if we tie into the Rio Hondo country.'

'And would they compare with the Rio Hondo country for good grazing land, and a clear right to the title?' asked Drinkwater.

'Maybe not, Boss. But they'd be a damned sight easier to handle.'

With a thrust like a duellist driving home his rapier Drinkwater shot the tip of the pointer once more into the centre of Rio Hondo County.

'Look here!' he snapped. 'This part of the Texas range is fine grazing land. It is held on a clear title by a clan, by three families for their services to Texas during the wars

* Told in *Quiet Town*, by J. T. Edson.

10

with Mexico and after. Their strength lies in their unity and I plan to destroy that unity, set them at each other's throats, then move in and take the pickings, just as we did in Uvalde. Uvalde was the testing ground, Bill, the training ground where we learned the technique. Now we know how to do it and we can go after the plum prize. The Rio Hondo country. I need your help, Bill.'

'I'm sorry, Boss,' Acre replied, shaking his head. 'Any other place I'd go for. But not Rio Hondo County. It's just not worth the risk.'

Drinkwater shrugged his shoulders. 'Very well, Bill, I go on my own.'

'Does that mean we're finished, Boss?'

'No. Go back to Uvalde and run things until you see that I've the situation in hand. Then you can come down and take over.'

'I can make the westbound if I go now,' Acre replied, glancing at the clock.

'Very well. Do you need any expenses?'

'Got all I need, thanks, Boss.'

With that Acre walked towards the door, took up his hat and set it right on his head. Just before he left the room, the big man turned to Drinkwater and made a last try at preventing what he knew to be a grave mistake.

'Don't do it, Boss,' he said.

He turned and left the room. Now it all depended on Drinkwater, he mused as he walked towards the main doors of the building. He had given his warning and he could do no more. Drinkwater was right about one thing, the way the Hardin, Fog and Blaze families came by their land. It had been given to them for their part in the fight to free Texas from Mexican rule. They did not receive the land for sitting on their butt-ends and talking, but for fighting, guts and hard, cold courage.

Acre was walking along the drive towards the gates when a fine looking coach pulled in. A beautiful face peered at him in passing and he nodded a greeting but did not return to speak with the guests. He hoped that they might talk sense into his boss.

'Mr. and Miss Defluer to see you, sir.'

Drinkwater turned as his butler entered the room. He walked forward to greet his guests with a smile of welcome on his face. Nor was the welcome feigned, one put on for clients, for Drinkwater genuinely liked Aristes Defluer and felt more than a liking for the man's daughter.

The girl who entered the room on her father's arm was beautiful. Her raven black hair, cared for at the hands of a master in tonsorial art, framed a face as near perfection as a man could ask for. Her figure appeared faultless and the green dress under her evening cloak showed it to full effect. Paulette Defluer not only looked beautiful but had been trained to do all the things a lady of her class needed to know. She could keep a conversation going even if she did not understand it, using the words yes and no to great effect. She could act as hostess at a dinner party, organise a house party, rode side-saddle very well, discuss art, music or the theatre with the air of one who knows what it is about.

Her chief charm in Drinkwater's eyes was that she, while an inch taller than himself, contrived to make him feel he stood much taller than her.

Having removed her cloak, Paulette swept forward, offering a cheek for him to kiss. To match her dress the jewellery she wore had an emerald motif, worn with just the correct amount of splendour to remain good taste. The green of the dress set off the smooth white of her arms and bosom, and filled Drinkwater with yearning.

Aristes Defluer was a big, heavily built man, inclined to be pompous and a trifle overbearing. In a lesser person this might have been regarded as a serious social failing, but Defluer carried it off with the air of a man who had the power to make or break a business with a word or pen stroke. On Wall Street Defluer's name spelt power and wealth. He was always on the lookout for other ways in which to increase his fortune and there were few shrewder operators on the stock exchange than Drinkwater's visitor. Defluer's clothes were cut to the height of fashion and he appeared as much at home in the room as Acre had looked out of place.

'I just saw Mr. Acre,' Paulette said, disengaging herself from Drinkwater's arms and moving back with a smile. 'He looked positively grumpy.'

Due to the arrival in New York of several members of the British aristocracy all Paulette's social set had adopted

English words and sayings. Paulette was ever in the fore-front of any new social development as she showed in her way of speaking.

'He's worried that we might have trouble during our vacation in Texas,' replied Drinkwater.

Delight showed in Paulette's eyes. 'You mean you have persuaded Papa to forget his old business and take me on vacation. That's absolutely ripping.'

'I think I might have,' smiled Drinkwater, for he knew Defluer's weakness. The man could refuse his daughter nothing.

'When do we leave?' she asked.

'On Monday. Travel west to Chicago, then down to Texas on one of the branch lines. From there by stage to Diggers Wells.'

'On Monday?' she almost shrieked. 'That's impossible. I haven't a thing to wear.'

'I'm sure you've something,' Drinkwater replied. 'Some little thing. You know how it is with businessmen, dear. If we stay any longer there's a chance either your father or I might become involved in some deal which will take weeks to clear and so lose our chance of getting away.'

Drinkwater showed his considerable knowledge of human nature in that the argument he used would be the one most likely to win Paulette over. The girl wanted to see his ranch in Texas very much, so much she would be will-ing to select from her considerable wardrobe to make the journey instead of having an entirely new outfit tailored, which would take time and might cost her the trip.

'Very well,' she said. 'I'll do as you say. Of course there won't be any of our set there so it won't really matter.'

'Where would you like to go tonight?' he asked.

'How about Harry Miller's café?' Paulette replied.

The two men exchanged startled glances and Drinkwater asked, 'Where did you hear about Miller's place?'

'All the girls have been talking about it. They're posi-tively gloating because I haven't been there.'

'Then Miller's it is,' Drinkwater chuckled. 'Now pop off and do what you ladies do before going out. I want to talk with your father.'

Paulette could take a hint and left the room. The two men faced each other and Drinkwater poured out a couple

13

of drinks.

'Acre doesn't think too highly of our plans,' he told the financier.

'*Your* plans, Basil. I'm in no way committed as yet. I don't like it, if Acre has turned you down.'

'You haven't had the experience I have with these westerners,' Drinkwater pointed out. 'They hear a story, embroider on it, pass it around, until a commonplace killer becomes regarded as something like an avenging angel and more deadly than bubonic plague. Acre's brave enough, but he's also intelligent enough to have just enough imagination to believe in fairy tales.'

'You're asking me to throw in a large sum,' answered Defluer. 'More than I can afford with the current state of the market.'

'One of the Rio Hondo men is Captain Dusty Fog.'

'C-Captain Dusty Fog?' croaked Defluer, allowing his glass to fall unheeded to the floor. 'You mean . . .'

'I mean the man who killed your son during the war.'

All too well Drinkwater knew the story of Aristes Defluer junior. In the War Between The States the young man, Defluer's only son, had insisted on joining the Union Army. With his father's backing he became a captain in the volunteer regiment without such formalities as West Point training, rising from lowly second lieutenant and learning his military duties on the way up.

The volunteer regiment armed themselves with lances, weapons which looked remarkably efficient and war-like— on a parade ground—and were ideal for tent-pegging, skewering pieces of wood buried into the ground and picked up in passing, from the back of a horse. The officers became adept at this pastime for they were rich young bloods who had the benefit of learning to ride almost as soon as they could walk. The enlisted men did not have this advantage for few had ever ridden horses before joining. They were still learning to ride when the regiment went into action—they were also the only members of the regiment armed with lances in combat, the officers carrying sabres and Colt 1860 Army revolvers.

Under such circumstances there could only be one result. In their first meeting with well organised and trained Southern cavalry they were routed and broken. Among the dead left on the battlefield was one Captain Aristes Defluer —he had been shot in the back.

After the war ended Defluer senior called in the aid of the newly formed Pinkerton Detective Agency to discover how his son came to die. The Lancer Volunteers had disbanded after their one battle, its records were lost and the members scattered. At last the agent in charge of the investigation located and produced a man who not only fought in the battle, but retained a surprising memory of details about the fight. He swore it was the battalion commanded by Captain Dusty Fog which fell on them treacherously from the rear and he had actually seen the rebel leader put a bullet into young Aristes' back. His description was vivid, telling how the huge, bearded, uncouth southerner on a huge white stallion charged down on them and pistolled Artistes from behind, roaring with laughter as he did so.

From this graphic description, the validity of which neither Defluer nor the Pinkerton man troubled to check, the financier formed a picture of a man, black bearded, savage looking and taking sadistic pleasure in butchering Union troops, especially his only son. The feeling never left Defluer, the hate was always with him, more so when alone in his office and he looked across at the empty desk where his son should have sat on his return from the war. His hatred for Captain Dustine Edward Marsden Fog grew, although he never tried to exact revenge.

Drinkwater knew of this hate. No man could be a friend of Defluer for more than three days without hearing the story of how Aristes Defluer junior came to die. He hoped this hate might be the lever which would throw Defluer's lot in with his own for the forthcoming operation showed signs of being costly.

'What are your plans?' Defluer asked.

'First we go down to the ranch, so you can see I haven't misrepresented any of the facts. We still stay there until the New Year. Your absence from town on vacation at such a time should help steady the market.'

Defluer sat back in his chair for a moment and gave the matter some thought. His presence in the city was always noted, especially in times of crisis. If he left on vacation it might have the effect of calming down the restive spirits or

15

the nervous ones among the speculators. Nobody would expect him to leave town unless all was well.

'We'll do it,' he finally said.

At that moment his daughter returned and business was forgotten in the preparation for the visit to Harry Miller's saloon. They took Drinkwater's comfortable coach to make the journey.

In the coach Drinkwater said little, but he was thinking of cattle and money. Since the war the western lands had developed the cattle industry into one of the great money-gatherers in the country. Fortunes were being made in Texas from the beef cattle which grazed on thousands of square miles of open range. The money found its way into the hands of southerners, men who fought against the Union in the Civil War. Drinkwater was no blind patriot, he harboured dreams of trying to stop the south becoming powerful enough to re-raise the Stars and Bars. He had established his fortune while other men rode to glory and fame of war and might have become richer had the south held on longer. Now he saw a chance to cut in on the money-making cattle industry and he intended to make the most of his chance.

It would not be easy. Acre's attitude proved that. Acre, bold, reckless and, in Drinkwater's eastern eyes, fast with his gun, yet he would not face the men of the Rio Hondo country.

One answer would be to hire eastern toughs, men from Brooklyn, the Bronx or Chicago's Badlands. They would be fighting men and unafraid of Texas reputations. Yet they would not know cowhand ways. What he needed was a man who knew cowhands, a man from the west who was unafraid of the Rio Hondo's families.

'I need a man!'

Drinkwater gave a guilty start, realising that he had spoken aloud for the last few words. Paulette, at his side, was staring at him with puzzled eyes.

'You want a *what*, dear?' she asked.

'I'm sorry, Paulette. I was thinking aloud. It's a bad fault. And I've been neglecting you. Look that's Harry Miller's place down there.'

'Is it Amazon tonight?' she asked.

'No, you've no need to worry. Miller's place is as well run

as Delmonico's.'

Paulette's lips pouted a little. She was disappointed that she would not see the entertainment known as Amazon Night, for all her friends had witnessed it and she hated to feel left out of anything.

CHAPTER TWO

JOHNNY RAYBOLD IN THE CITY

All in all, Johnny Raybold found New York to be something of a disappointment after his anticipation of the visit. The tall young Texan, one time scout for the Wedge trail drive crew, had been in the big city for three days and found little that any of the trail end towns could not offer. There were crowds, more people than Johnny could ever remember seeing together at one time, there was bustle and noise. But he found none of the friendly atmosphere of the west.

Not that Johnny was a naïve country yokel in the big city. He had a shrewd idea that his companion, the pretty Josie Kilroy, was less interested in him than in his well filled wallet. He accepted that. It was just one of the risks a man took in life, happen he rode on trail drives for a living. So Johnny aimed to have a good time and make the most of Josie's company as he'd done with calico cats in a dozen towns, they being the only female company a cowhand on the trail was likely to meet. Josie was pretty enough, not too obviously what she was, she laughed, talked and had fun. More than that, she steered him from the rather dead place in which they met and brought him to Harry Miller's garish establishment.

'You've never seen anything like it, Johnny,' she promised as they entered the downstairs bar-room.

It seemed Josie was not unused to entering such places. She led the way to the bar instead of a table. The girl was pretty, her red hair taken up in a pile on top of the head, her face just painted enough to make her attractive. She stood around five four at most and had a rich, full, plump figure. Yet he had felt the strength in her arms, the hard muscles under the smooth skin. These came as no surprise to him, girls of Josie's kind often had to work hard and

18

developed strength beyond that of their more leisurely and fortunate sisters. She walked with a light-footed, graceful step which showed there was little flabby fat on her plump body and the mauve dress she wore fitted tight enough to show the firm curves under it.

She looked like the sort of girl Johnny would go for at the end of a long drive, pleasant and good company. Yet she appeared to have picked him out soon after he entered Duke Daniel's place further down-town, leaving the group of men who had been sitting with her on his arrival.

'I like tall men,' she had told him when joining him at the bar.

Well, Johnny was tall. He stood just over six foot and had wide shoulders, a lean waist and a body bursting with muscular health and vitality. His low crowned, wide brimmed Stetson had sat Texas style on a thatch of fiery red hair. His face was tanned, handsome, showed intelligence and strength of will. It would have taken something a whole heap more powerful than the polite conventions of the east to make Johnny Raybold wear a closed collar or a tie. His shirt neck stayed open, the tight rolled blue bandana hung long ends down over this leather jacket which was fastened for a very good reason. His levis trousers hung cowhand style outside his high-heeled, fancy stitched boots. Taken all in all, Johnny could be nothing but what he was. A Texas cowhand on a spree.

'What'll it be, honey?' he asked.

'Wine,' she replied in a half-hearted way.

From the way Josie now acted, and from practical experience, Johnny got the idea the girl was waiting for something, or somebody. Her eyes repeatedly flickered up to the bar mirror to study the scene behind her. Johnny grinned. This could be a badger game he had let himself in for. In that case when her protector arrived Josie would suggest they went to her room. Once they were settled down an enraged 'husband' would burst in demanding money or satisfaction for the defection of Josie. If this was the old badger game Johnny allowed to make the badger wish he had stayed in bed. Johnny was something of a catch-dog where human badgers were concerned, and he, in the Texas term, was fully dressed at this moment.

However, caution cost nothing. So Johnny also watched

the mirror. He saw four of the men who had been with Josie in the other place enter Miller's. They did not come as a group, but singly and mingled among the crowd. That was a tolerable amount of weight for the badger game, although they might play it different in New York, or maybe figured a Texas cowhand needed more men to handle than did a dude from the city.

Josie gave no sign of wishing to leave, but she still darted glances at the mirror.

A blonde girl carrying a tray walked towards them along the front of the bar. Johnny studied her reflection in the mirror. She was much the same height as Josie, maybe an inch smaller and a few odd pounds heavier. She was pretty in an open, coarse way and laughed at the greetings called to her. The brief outfit she wore left little to be imagined and showed off her plump figure.

This was not the first time the girl passed and Johnny watched her in the mirror's reflection as she served the tables of the big tippers and lavish spenders. He saw the way the other girls gave way before the blonde and knew enough saloon girls to figure she must either have the boss's favour or be tough enough to handle any objections to her taking the plum tables all the time.

'I'm just going out back, Johnny,' Josie said.

She turned and crashed full into the blonde. The tray tilted up, glasses flew from it and liquor splashed over both of them.

'You clumsy cow!' Josie spat the words out.

'Watch where you're going, you fat whore!' hissed the blonde in the same breath.

Josie's hand swung around. The flat 'splat' of the slap sounded loud and the blonde staggered back. Johnny, who had turned, winced in sympathy. That had been some bare-handed slap and it left angry fingermarks on the blonde's cheek. She staggered back a few paces, hit a table and hung on to it for a moment.

Then she forced herself away from it. All around the room customers came to their feet, the band stopped, the singer on the stage halted in mid-chord. Every eye went to the blonde. She started forward, fists clenched and held ready for use, moving in a half crouch after a style Johnny had never seen before. Josie faced her, standing erect, fingers ready to dig into hair, or claw at flesh.

A big man burst forward, coming down the stairs leading to the balcony area where the upper class visitors had their tables away from the common herd. He was clearly a man of importance dressed in his own idea of how a gentleman should. His derby hat was of the stylish model with a curly brim, his suit a loud check and his polka dot bow-tie clashed with a sickly looking pink shirt. His face was red and coarse, his voice a hoarse bellow as he charged forward.

'Nah then! Nah then!' he bellowed. 'What's all this abaht?'

The blonde girl halted in her tracks, keeping her fists up ready. Johnny caught Josie by the arms, feeling the hard, firm muscles under the skin even more now. She strained against him slightly, still glaring at the blonde.

'Cawn't have carryings on like this here!' went on the big man. 'This's a respectable sporting club, not a cat house. Nah then, Carrie, what happened?'

'She turned and bumped into me deliberately, Harry,' replied the blonde.

'You're a liar!' Josie yelled back. 'You swerved at me. I'll scratch your eyes out, you fat cow. Let me at her, Johnny, I'll snatch her bald-headed.'

'Nah hold hard there, young woman!' interrupted the man, who could only be Harry Miller, Johnny figured. He threw a look at the expectant crowd. 'You want to settle this with Carrie?'

'Just let me at her and I'll show you!' Josie screamed back.

'All right then. We'll put you two ladies in the ring with the gloves on right after the next act.'

Johnny wasn't sure what the man meant. He saw the mocking sneer mingled in with the hate on Carrie's face and got the idea whatever was meant it would not be pleasant for Josie.

'Hold hard there a minute,' he began. 'What's all this about?'

'Just a chance for the ladies to let off steam,' replied Miller with an ingratiating grin on his face. 'Nobody'll get hurt.'

'It's all right, Johnny,' Josie went on. 'I'll show that fat cow where she comes off.'

This was what Miller hoped she would say. He had studied the girl with suspicious eyes when she first entered into the trouble with Carrie. Now he thought her to be a member of the oldest profession freshly arrived in New York and unaware of where she was. In that case it would be so much better. Miller knew what a draw a fight between two girls could be. His saloon ran what he termed Amazon Night every Friday, with girl boxers playing at sparring, although they sometimes fought seriously. He could see that this spontaneous bout might form a good attraction for the red-head looked as if her temper might keep her going for longer than when one of his own girls was matched against Carrie. That would give the crowd a good show and boost sales at the bar, for watching girl fights seemed to have a salutary effect on the thirst of the customers.

'That your gal?' asked a man, coming to Johnny's side as Josie strolled away towards the rear of the building, following Miller and the girl called Carrie.

'Nope, just some gal I met,' Johnny replied, seeing Miller stop and talk to a waiter, pointing towards the bar.

'That's all right then,' the man went on. ''Cause when Carrie Wells finishes with her she won't look very pretty.'

Even in three days stay in New York Johnny had heard of Carrie Wells, although he had not connected her with the blonde waitress. Her photograph, or a sketch of her, appeared in every barber's shop and a number of saloons, posing in a brief and revealing outfit, with strange looking gloves on her hands. She was called the Lady Boxing Champion of America. Johnny did not know what boxing was, what he had seen had been done with bare fists and was called pugilism, or just plain fist-fighting. He had wondered about the way she was illustrated standing something like a pugilist, now he knew why.

'Boss sent you this,' said the bartender, placing a bottle of whisky and a glass by Johnny's elbow.

'Why for?' asked Johnny.

'Didn't want you feeling out of it now your gal's gone. Said if you fancied any of the waitresses to say the word and he'd have her called over.'

'Kind of him,' growled Johnny.

The bartender leaned across the polished mahogany surface. 'Look, cowboy, don't you try to stop it now it's got this far. This ain't Dodge City, nor yet the Badlands of Chicago. You cause Harry Miller fuss you're likely to wind up face down in the East River looking as if a bad horse stomped you.'

Johnny had been thinking of trying to get Josie out of the room, but he knew the voice of experience when he heard it.

'What do you-all reckon I should do, mister?'

'Drink your drink and let it go by. Carrie'll clip your gal around the ear a few times. Then your gal'll either start to bawl and want out, or she'll hit the canvas for a ten count and it'll be all over.'

'I don't read that brand,' Johnny drawled. 'What's this here ten count?'

'It's the new fist fighting rules, call it boxing. They wear padded gloves, fight three minute rounds with a minute's rest between each round, instead of until one of 'em gets knocked down. If one gets knocked down she has to be on her feet afore the referee counts to ten. If she don't it's the same as if she couldn't toe the line after time in a knock-down bout.'

'You mean fellers are fighting to them rules now?' asked Johnny.

'They sure are,' grinned the bartender. 'It's turned pugilism into a real sissy game.'

So Johnny relaxed. If what the bartender said was true Josie shouldn't get too badly hurt. Unless, as he suspected, there was a lot more to Josie than met the eye.

In one of the side boxes overlooking the big room Drinkwater and his party had been watching everything. It made a change from the singer who gamely tried to finish his act on the stage despite the noise made from behind the curtain as Miller's men erected the boxing ring.

Paulette Defluer turned a disappointed face to Drinkwater as the two girls followed Miller from the room. All her friends had seen a boxing bout at Miller's saloon, it was one of the things to be done this season, like visiting the opera, or attending some newly discovered painter's exhibition. Paulette was disappointed if the one slap was all it amounted to.

'Is that all there is to it?' she asked. 'All my friends made

23

a boxing match sound so much more interesting.'

'The girls have gone to change for the match,' Drink-water replied. 'We'll see the bout after the singer finishes his act, won't we, Aristes?'

Defluer jerked back as if startled by the words. He had been sat on the edge of his chair and straining down at the stage, although not out of interest in the singer. He swung to face the other two.

'Disgusting business,' he said. 'You should take Paulette out of here before the degrading spectacle begins, Basil.'

'Oh no, Papa!' Paulette wailed. 'All my friends have seen a female boxing bout here, I feel so out of it!'

'Very well then, stay,' replied Defluer, who had no intention of leaving and missing the disgusting and degrading spectacle himself. In fact he was a regular visitor on Amazon Nights and always had this box at the edge of the stage so he could be sure of the best possible view of the entire affair.

Drinkwater looked across the room to where Johnny stood alone at the bar. That hat style looked familiar and the man's clothes were certainly not those of a city dweller.

'That man who was with the red-head,' he said. 'He's a cowhand of some sort. I'm not sure, but I think he's a Texas man.'

'They sometimes come east,' replied Defluer, less interested in the crowd than in the forthcoming and disgusting spectacle.

'I suppose so,' Drinkwater answered, then joined in the polite applause as the singer finished his act. 'Well, that's over, Paulette. You'll soon see your boxing match now.'

CHAPTER THREE

CARRIE'S MISTAKE

An expectant hush fell over the saloon as the curtains drew back to show the ring which would be used for the forthcoming fight. Johnny Raybold looked it over with interest for he had seen such things rarely, most bare-fists bouts did not have such elaborate fittings. The square had been erected by Miller's men in record time, including the four corner posts which supported the taunt trip ropes. In one corner stood a medium sized, slim man wearing stylish trousers and a frilly bosomed white shirt, the collar open and sleeves rolled up. At the side of the ring sat a man with a gong and mallet on a small table and a watch in his hand. Johnny guessed he must be responsible for starting and ending the rounds.

Then the two girls came on to the stage from opposite sides. Carrie Wells had merely removed the brief skirt from her working clothes and changed from her high-heeled shoes into a pair of calf high, heel-less boots. From the way the brief bodice clung to her she wore nothing underneath it. Two men followed her, each carrying a pair of the padded gloves, one also carried a bucket and the other a towel.

Josie walked forward and ducked between the ropes at the other side. She had her street cloak draped around her shoulders, but underneath wore a similar outfit to Carrie's and on her feet were the same sort of heel-less boots as Carrie's, with little red tassels on top. She stood alone in the corner of the ring.

From his place at the bar, Johnny studied the girl. He felt even more certain this entire business was pre-arranged in some way. On leaving the other saloon Johnny had noticed the girl wore those same heel-less boots with the red tassels but thought nothing of it as he did not know if such formed

25

part of a lady's dress fashion in New York. He watched Josie, she seemed just too at home in the way she acted.

Now Miller was on the stage and waving the crowd to silence.

'Ladies and gentlemen!' he bellowed. 'You all know me. Fair play's my motto. Now I'm asking any of you gents as have handled prize-fighters, two of you, to come up here and handle the challenger.'

Two men rose hurriedly from the audience, beating a few others. They headed for the stage to jeers and ribald comments from the less fortunate members of the crowd. The men were seconds who worked around the training camps of the boxers, for many such came to Miller's place and there was always a chance of getting this sort of job, acting for one of the girls.

With a bored air Carrie Wells held out her hands for the boxing gloves to be laced on. She threw a mocking smile at Josie, thinking of the licking she aimed to hand to the rash red-head.

For her part Josie looked relaxed. One of her seconds collected a pair of gloves from Carrie's corner. The other second checked the bucket and bottle of water in the ring corner, but did not touch it yet. He removed Josie's cloak and put it outside the ring, then helped lace the gloves on Josie's hands.

'If you've the feeling to bet on your gal, cowhand,' said the bartender to Johnny, 'you'll find plenty to take you.'

'Will, huh?'

'Sure. Only you'd be wasting your money. You could get odds of four or five to one against your gal.'

Looking across the room Johnny saw one of the men who had been with Josie in the other saloon. The man appeared to be making a sizeable bet with one of the house gamblers.

'That referee feller,' Johnny drawled, nodding to where the official was examining the girls' gloves as they stood with him in the centre of the ring. 'He work for your boss?'

'Naw. That's Mr. Lou Craddle. He's the top referee in town. Always handles the bouts here if he's in. Can't say I blame him, right in there among the girls and having a good view of everything.'

The referee stood by the girls and had finished his check

of their gloves. Harry Miller stood in the ring and the crowd fell silent.

'And now for your entertainment!' he bellowed. 'A twelve three minute round bout of boxing between the Lady Champion of the World, our own Carrie Wells!'

Carrie acknowledged the cheers of the crowd with confidence, then returned to her corner and leaned on the ropes, watching Josie all the time with the same mocking smile.

'And the challenger. From Detroit. Josie Kilroy!'

Josie turned around, showing off her figure in the borrowed bodice. Once more Johnny was aware of the feeling that Josie knew what all this was about. She did not act like a girl wild with anger and wanting to tangle in a hair-yanking brawl. Yet on the gong sounding she showed no sign of knowing what to do. She stepped forward from her corner with her hands hanging at her sides. Carrie came dancing out, crouching slightly, stabbing blows in the manner of shadow-boxing. She looked like a girl who knew the game from A to izzard and ought to be an easy winner.

Watching Josie move from her corner of the ring Johnny Raybold got the idea she was not going to be the easy meat Carrie Wells expected. Carrie came dancing out, fists up and throwing a right at Josie's face. Then Josie dropped her pose. She weaved aside, left hand deflecting the blow over her shoulder. Her right fist shot out to drive into Carrie's middle and fold the blonde girl over. On the heels of the blow Josie threw up a punch with her left, the glove smashing into the down-dropping jaw. The crowd yelled its surprise as Carrie went over backwards to crash on to the padded canvas of the floor.

After throwing a startled glance at first Josie then Carrie, the referee began to count. Carrie rolled over on to her stomach, gasping and shaking her head as she forced herself to hands and knees. At seven she made her feet. Her eyes glowed with hate as she moved into the attack once more.

Only she moved with caution, alert and watchful. The two punches had landed hard, shaking her badly and she knew she needed to watch the other girl. Now Carrie could see that Josie was no street girl who had wandered into the saloon and been suckered into the ring to be thrashed for the amusement of Miller's customers. The red-head was dancing lightly on her toes, fists up in the recognised style for boxing, showing she knew the game. Carrie felt rage boiling heavily inside her. Not only could her opponent box but Josie had landed two good punches which would weigh heavily in her favour in the fight which they both knew lay ahead.

Suddenly Josie flew forward. Left, right, left, right. Her fists shot out, landing hard on Carrie's face and body, driving the blonde back across the ring. Carrie backed away, throwing out her right hand to try and hold back the other girl for she had been taken aback by the ferocity of the attack and the power behind the blows.

Josie weaved, bent, then smashed home another blow into Carrie's stomach. Once more the crowd yelled and groaned as their favourite collapsed to the floor holding her body and writhing while she tried to gasp in air.

At eight Carrie made her feet. Even as Josie came forward to attack once more Carrie sank to one knee to the canvas. The referee began his count, reaching seven before Carrie forced herself up. She seemed to have regained her breath but she backed away. Having twice sampled the power of Josie's body punches Carrie knew the danger of them.

The surprise attack, the savage blows handed to her before she was ready, or expected to take them, shook Carrie. Josie forced home her advantage with a savage double-handed attack on the other girl. Three more times during the round Carrie went to the floor. Once she dropped to one knee in an attempt to avoid punishment. On the other occasions it was Josie's lashing fists which sent her sprawling to smell the resin. Much to everyone's surprise the round very clearly went to Josie. Carrie looked relieved as the bell sounded to send her into the corner for a rest and a chance to gather her wits.

She gained a little from the rest. Yet the surprise handed to her, the way she caught the blows, left her dazed. It would take some time to shake off the effects of the blows, even if she could avoid taking any more punishment.

So the second round found Carrie boxing cautiously, using all her skill to keep out of trouble. Instead of her usual rushing tactics Carrie backed away, danced clear, fought a defensive battle. She kept her feet all that round and didn't go down once, or take a really punishing blow, but she had not landed four good punches by the time the gong ended round two.

'Was I you,' said the bartender to Johnny as they watched the seconds working on the girls at the end of round two, 'I'd start heading for the door.'

'Meaning?' Johnny drawled.

'Harry Miller isn't going to like you bringing a professional gal boxer in here to muss Carrie up.'

Johnny swung towards the man, meaning to frame an angry denial. Then he saw how this business must look to the people in the saloon. He also saw the reason for Josie picking him up and steering him into Harry Miller's place. She came here deliberately to pick a fight with Carrie Wells and get into the ring. The boots she wore proved that this had been arranged in advance. They were the pair she had worn when he met her and according to the bartender were the kind used for this new form of fist-fighting. It began to look as if Johnny had been set up like a stool-pigeon to keep suspicion from Josie. The men from the other place were here to make bets on a girl they apparently didn't know. If any blame for Josie's presence fell, it looked like it would land straight on Johnny's head.

A yell from the crowd brought Johnny's attention to the ring. The girls had come out once more and from the look of things Carrie was showing some of her old skill. She landed a right to the side of Josie's face, staggering the redhead backwards and jarring her upswept hair loose. Carrie followed up the punch with a savage two-handed attack which drove Josie around the ring. A left started a trickle of blood running from Josie's nose. A right cross rocked her head to one side. A brutal left to her ribs brought a gasp of pain, then the right smashed home and Josie hit the floor on her hands and knees. Wild with rage Carrie leapt forward and lashed a kick into Josie's ribs. Josie moaned, twisted around to lock her arms around Carrie's legs and bring her down. They rolled over and over on the floor. Now boxing was forgotten as they tried to grip hair with their gloved hands.

The crowd howled with laughter as the two girls rolled over and over. Craddle tried to separate them and called

29

the seconds to help. Between them they got the girls apart and on their feet.

In the box over the ring Paulette watched, fascinated but still believing it to be some kind of act.

'Are they allowed to do that?' she asked, when Carrie kicked Josie.

Drinkwater shook his head. 'No, but it would take a braver man than Referee Craddle to disqualify them. The crowd would lynch him if he stopped the bout now.'

Yet Drinkwater was worried. He could see this was not the usual Amazon Night tip and tap session and might not be a pretty sight by the time it ended. He wished he had not brought Paulette along this evening.

In the ring the two girls were separated. They stood gasping for breath and glaring at each other for an instant while Craddle warned them about such conduct. Both reverted to boxing again and the round ended without either gaining any clear advantage.

From his place at the edge of the stage Miller listened to the excited talk welling around him as the customers discussed the fight so far. He had merely said twelve rounds as a figure, not because he felt the red-head would last so long. Now it looked as if the fight would last longer than expected. He scowled across the room towards the tall cowhand at the bar. Such a man did not belong to any of the local gangs, of that Miller was sure. The saloon keeper had not failed to notice how Josie's style improved after the first blows of the fight. That girl was a trained boxer and very good with it. Perhaps she and the cowhand came to make a few dollars, or even a lot of dollars, after tricking Carrie into the ring.

With this thought in mind Miller called over the head of his house gamblers. He discovered that Johnny had not laid any bets, but that four men laid considerable amounts on Josie and at favourable odds.

For her part Carrie did not mind having the extra rounds. She hoped to wear down the other girl with her greater skill. Only after two more evenly fought and fast moving rounds she began to realise that her skill was not much greater than Josie's. Carrie looked thoughtful as she returned to her corner at the end of the sixth round.

Three more hard rounds followed. The girls fought with

a female primeval savagery and hate. Even the hardened girl-fight fans, and the workers of the saloon who had grown blasé about the bouts staged every week, grew silent as the girls tore into each other. Never before had any of them seen two women go at it in the ring with such pent-up fury.

Yet those early blows, taken before she had been ready in the first minute of the opening round, took their toll now. Carrie might have been excused for wishing the fight had been only for six rounds by the time she staggered out for the tenth. Her nose and mouth were bleeding, her eyes puffy and discoloured, blood running from a cut over one, but she would not allow the referee to rule her unfit to continue. Her shoulders, the bodice, legs and boots were splashed with her own and Josie's blood for not all the punishment had gone one way and the red-head was just as badly marked by now, although not quite so badly battered.

Through all the tenth round it was clear guts and hatred alone that kept Carrie on her feet. She stumbled into punches, clinched and tried to cling close to Josie so as to hold off the blows which smashed into her. Then it happened.

Once more the brutal right drove into Carrie's stomach, bringing a croak of agony and doubling her over. The left came to lift her erect, on her toes. Josie drove her right around, smashing against the side of Carrie's head and sending her across the ring to hang halfway through the ropes. Josie almost fell herself and hung on to the ropes for support. Every inch of her body felt raw and sick from swallowing blood and her ribs were as tender as a steak fresh from under the hands of a master chef. Craddle started his count, but it was plain to everyone that Carrie wouldn't rise.

Miller for one was sure. He caught the eye of the time-keeper and made a sign. The referee's hand was lifting for the eighth of the count and there was no time to lose. If Carrie could be saved she might possibly keep her feet until the end of the twelfth round when the fight could be declared a draw. Miller cared nothing for the suffering Carrie would go through in the next two rounds. His money was at stake and he hated losing money.

'Eight!' said the referee.

The gasp which rang from the customers rose high as the gong clanged, saving Carrie from being counted out. None of the watching crowd had kept a careful check of the time and did not know the gong sounded a full fifteen seconds early.

In the box Drinkwater threw a glance at Paulette as the second carried Carrie's limp body to the ring corner. After the first four rounds Paulette had said little or nothing, but just stared at the ring. Her face had lost most of its colour and her hands clenched until the knuckles showed white. He did not know if he should suggest they leave.

Both sets of seconds were working on their girls and the timekeeper allowed two minutes to tick by before he banged his gong. The extra time enabled the seconds to get Carrie on her feet, but it also allowed Josie to recover even more.

In desperation, trying to avoid the punishing fists, Carrie clinched, clinging to Josie's waist. They staggered across the ring and the referee tried to separate them. Josie struggled wildly and felt the hold released. She thrust hard and Carrie staggered backwards a few paces. With all the strength she had left Josie smashed Carrie in the stomach once more, then ripped up another punch which smashed home with a thud which sounded around the room. Carrie was flung back across the ring, her flailing arms hung over the top rope, her feet not touching the floor as she hung backwards.

Paulette let out a strangled gasp of horror. Carrie hung on the ropes just below the box. The blonde's head was thrown back, ashy, bloody and hideous looking with glazed eyes rolling sightlessly upwards as the bloodly mouth worked in soundless agony.

'Oh!' gasped Paulette. 'Get me out of here, Basil!'

Her friends had only seen the bouts on Amazon Nights, with the results arranged in advance and each round worked out like the steps of a dance routine. Even the few who had seen serious bouts had never seen one which went on with the savage brutal fury of this fight.

Although he was not a man easily moved by suffering Drinkwater felt sickened by what he witnessed that night. Even Defluer's face looked greenish and sick as he stared at the bloody wreck which slid slowly forward from the ropes while the referee counted and held Josie back from attacking again.

'Please get me out of here!' moaned Paulette.

Drinkwater rose and made a sign to his coachman, but the man, down at the side of the room, had his full attention on the ring. So Drinkwater led the girl from the box and left her in her father's care while he went to warn the coachman his party would need the coach soon.

The battered blonde slowly slid forward and crashed on to her face on the floor. Josie almost fell on to the ropes but stayed erect until the count was over. Then the referee took her hand, raised it into the air.

'The winner!' he said.

Josie did not hear him. Her legs buckled under and she slid to the floor of the ring to lie by the side of the woman she had tricked, fought and beaten.

CHAPTER FOUR

I'M NOT AFRAID OF DUSTY FOG

For a long time the bar-room stayed silent as the customers stared at the ring. Then, as her seconds went to help her rise again, Josie struggled to her hands and knees to the gradual accompaniment of cheering.

One of the house gamblers came to Miller's side and asked a question.

'Of course you've got to pay!' he snarled.

'There were four big bets, boss,' the man replied.

'You'll still have to pay,' Miller answered. 'We got too much of the quality in to chance a fight. Get going.'

In a fury he watched the bets being paid off and in the ring Josie was being helped through the ropes while Carrie's seconds lifted her up between them for it would be long before she recovered sufficiently to walk. Miller snarled to himself as he watched money changing hands, going out of his place. Yet there was no way of avoiding it. Not with his champion lying in the arms of her seconds, a bloody and defeated wreck and the girl who beat her walking unsteadily towards the dressing room.

A customer came towards Miller, a broad grin on his face and a handful of money in his hands.

'That red-headed gal sure took Carrie,' he said cheerfully. 'Reckon that's why Duke Daniels brought her into town.'

Miller's big hands shot out to grip the man by his lapels and thrust a big coarse face up to the other's scared visage.

'What do you mean?'

'I saw the gal in Duke's place earlier, with the four ginks who bet so heavily on her. They seemed real pally with Duke.'

Then Miller saw what had happened. He saw it a full five seconds to either stop the heavy betters leaving, or arrange to have them relieved of their ill-gotten gains outside. He swung around and headed for the dressing rooms, but was delayed by customers who wanted to congratulate him on the best fight they'd ever seen in the saloon. He charged down the steps towards the dressing rooms, almost knocking over the two men carrying Carrie in passing.

'Where is she?' he asked the pair of seconds who handled Josie.

'Feller had a carriage out back waiting for her,' one replied, waving a hand towards the rear door of the building. 'Didn't even wait to dress her, just got a blanket around her and took off.'

With a snarl of almost bestial fury Miller flung himself past the men carrying Carrie and headed for the bar-room. He cursed savagely and bitterly as he entered the room once more. Duke Daniels was a deadly rival, Miller's chief and most hated rival in the saloon business. The girl boxers Miller introduced had been an attraction Daniels was unable to top so far. Now it appeared that Daniels must have located the red-headed girl, trained her in secret and arranged the whole affair.

The mishap which caused the fight had been carefully arranged and planned. Miller and Carrie fell into the trap dug for them by Josie and Daniels. Miller's eagerness to make money by giving his customers a show, and Carrie's over-confidence regarding Josie as easy meat brought about their downfall. Before Carrie learned she had a skilled, trained fighter to contend with, not a hot-tempered street-girl, the savage blows landed and she never recovered fully from them.

Miller's eyes fell on the young cowhand who still stood at the bar and the saloon keeper's rage burst like the flood waters of a breached dam. He crossed the room to stand behind Johnny, nostrils flaring and head bowed slightly like a wild old bull pawing up dirt before it made its charge.

'I thought you'd've run out with the girl!' Miller snarled.

Cat-cautious and watchful, Johnny turned. He knew now that Josie only used him as an excuse to get into Miller's place and set up the fight. The girl had to have an escort to enter the saloon and she would not wish her friends to become too involved with her. So she must have been waiting for a likely pigeon to come into Daniels' place—and

35

Johnny had been that pigeon. Only he was damned if he aimed to run like a Mexican taking a greaser stand-off when all he had done was fall for a sucker trick.

'Now what you meaning, mister?' he asked.

'You and Daniels got this whole thing rigged between you. That chippy was a ringer you brought in here to make me lose money!'

'You got your lines twisted, mister,' Johnny replied evenly. 'I never set eyes on Josie afore this evening.'

Which same would have figured, made good sense and saved Miller some grief had he not been so wild-hot with rage. He wanted to take his hate out on somebody and overlooked the fact that had Johnny been in on the plot he would be unlikely to remain and face the consequences. So at the young Texan he unleashed all his hate. This proved to be unfortunate—for Miller.

Miller's big fist lashed out at Johnny's head. The saloon keeper knew much about fist-fighting and coached all his girls personally. His blow had been thrown with all his skill, it carried weight and power behind it. Miller expected to crash the fist into Johnny's face with enough strength to fell an ox.

Only at the last instant Johnny's head wasn't there any more. The Texan also knew something of fist-fighting and he sure didn't aim to stand there and take a punch which packed the power of a Missouri knob-head mule's kick.

With all his weight behind the blow, and confident it would land on flesh, Miller was caught off balance when he missed. Johnny took a page from Josie's book and ripped home a punch right where it would do the most good, full into Miller's belly. Softened by good living, too much rich food, drink and womanising, Miller could no longer take blows down there in anything like his old manner. He let out a croaking gasp and doubled forward. Johnny lashed up his knee, driving it into Miller's face and sprawling the man over on to his back.

Miller lit down spitting blood, then sat up and homicidal rage showed on his face as he howled, 'Get him!'

Eager to show Miller how tough he was, a man came up from his table. He shot a hand into his pocket and brought it out with Tammany mittens glinting brassy support to the power of his hard knuckles. He started forward, the brass knuckles set to rip flesh from Johnny's face.

Near to Johnny's hand stood the bottle of whisky given earlier by Miller. Up until then Johnny had been watching the fight and not bothered about drinking. Now he could see a real good use for the bottle and his hand closed on the neck. Whipping up the bottle Johnny hurled it forward with all his strength. The flying bottle smashed full into the big man's face, shattering and sprawling him back on top of Miller with blood rushing and mingling with the whisky on his face.

Then Johnny took off for the doors. Men scattered before him like the branding crew before the rush of a pain-enraged longhorn steer. A bouncer charged forward, head down and arms extended to grab. Johnny slowed down just at the right time. The bouncer shot before him, unable to stop, his head smashed into the front of the bar, which proved the stronger judging by the limp way he collapsed.

Johnny knew better than allow himself to become boxed in, for he had seen bad saloons before and had a shrewd idea of his fate if he allowed himself to be trapped inside. He opened his jacket as he ran, leaving free access to the walnut grips of the old 1860 Army Colt riding in his waist band.

Only one more man tried to stop Johnny, leaping forward with arms held ready to grab. The Texan had never seen a game of football in his life, but he might have both seen and played from the way he kicked on the run. The sharp toe of his riding boot caught the man full in the pit of his stomach, jack-knifed him over and sent him reeling to one side.

'Get him, damn you all!' screamed Miller, thrusting the unconscious man from him. 'I want his guts!'

By this time Johnny had reached the doors and went through them, into the open and all but deserted street. He lit down in the street just as Drinkwater's coach turned from out of the vacant lot next to Miller's, used for parking the vehicles of visiting gentry. Johnny saw the startled faces of the coach's occupants and the scared features of the coachman. Then he had troubles again.

A shot rang out. The whiplash crack of a light calibre Smith and Wesson, or a cheap suicide special. Whichever it was the bullet hissed by his head and a light calibre gun could kill as good as a .44 Army's ball at close range. The shooter missed, which was not the best thing to do when dealing with a man who had trailed cattle for the Wedge and learned real early how to handle a shooting iron. The man with the gun did not know this. He only wanted to earn Miller's gratitude and approbation by bringing down the trouble-causer. Which same was a hawg-stupid game for a New York tough to be playing against a Tejano who knew guns from his teeth-cutting days.

Johnny came around faster than a greased burned cat leaving a room. He fetched out that sleek, streamlined old Army Colt faster than the big city men bunched in the doorway had ever seen it done before. Flame lashed from the barrel and the man with the gun spun around, then went down, a .44 ball smashing his collar bone, in which he might count himself lucky for Johnny had not been meaning such fancy shooting as all that. The rest of the men at the doors dived back inside, but Johnny allowed they would soon be back and loaded for bear.

In that case, happen he aimed to stay alive long enough to grow all old and ornery, Johnny figured he had best put some distance between him and Miller's place. Only he did not know the range hereabouts, not like the city dudes inside, and the streets looked awful open to a man who wanted cover to hide behind and make a fight.

Like a good New York citizen Drinkwater's coachman did not wait for orders when he saw the trouble ahead. He applied a flick of the whip to his spirited team and they laid into the harness with a will, jerking the coach forward at a good speed. He sent the coach forward, passing the front of Miller's saloon and offering Johnny a much needed chance.

There was no time to respect the polite conventions. Johnny turned and sprang forward, gripping and opening the coach door, then hauling himself hurriedly inside. Defluer fell back in his seat as Johnny entered. Staring at the smoking Colt in Johnny's hand, Paulette flung her arms around Drinkwater's neck, clinging to him and effectively preventing him making a move, even if he aimed to try.

'Howdy, folks,' drawled Johnny. 'Sorry to horn in on you-all like this. But those boys back there were surely getting strenuous in their hospitality. I'll drop off again soon as I'm clear of their range.'

He set the hammer of his Colt on its safety notch, then thrust the revolver back into his waistband. Then he turned towards the girl and grinned in his most winning manner. When Johnny Raybold got the grin on his face no woman, be she old or young, ever felt she need be afraid of him.

'Right sorry if I scared you, ma'am,' he went on. 'Only those boys back to the saloon, they took to blaming me for the whupping their gal got from Josie.'

At that moment the coachman threw back his view slot and peered in. Drinkwater made a sign and the man closed the slot to concentrate on driving. Behind and around sounded police whistles and the drumming of night-sticks on railings or the pavement. The sound of shooting had attracted the law, but no policeman aimed to arrive on the scene unless he had plenty of backing.

'How did you happen to get tied in with this business?' Drinkwater asked.

'Met Josie down the street a piece, at the Lion's Den.'

'Duke Daniels' place?'

'Why sure. Anyways she got to talking, allowed we ought to see the sights and headed me along to Miller's. Happen I'd know what was going to come off I could've steered her clear. Or kept out of it myself.'

'It was ghastly!' Paulette put in, her face still pallid and sick looking. 'Those women—the way they—all that blood —I've never seen anything so brutal or terrible.'

'Yes, ma'am,' agreed Johnny. 'That was some whirl. Made the battle at Bearcat Annie's* look like a parson's Sunday School treat.'

None of the others had ever heard of the great fight in Bearcat Annie's saloon when three townswomen and the girls of the establishment battled it out toe to toe in a brawl which was still remembered throughout the west.

'You sound like a Texas man,' Drinkwater remarked, wanting to change the subject.

'Man'd say you called it right, friend,' Johnny agreed.

'Do you know the Rio Hondo country?'

'Why sure. That's where that pesky Dusty Fog and his kin hang out.'

'You don't like him from the way you speak,' Drinkwater went on.

* Told in *The Fastest Gun in Texas*, by J. T. Edson.

39

'I sure don't. One time I run him clear out of Abilene,' drawled Johnny, straight-faced and sober sounding.

Drinkwater studied Johnny for a long moment. He had not failed to notice the speed with which the Texan drew and shot with his long barrelled Colt. To Drinkwater's eyes the move had been faster than the way Acre fetched out his gun and sent lead into a target. More important, this tall young man was not afraid of the reputation of Dusty Fog and had actually driven the Rio Hondo gun-wizard out of a town.

'You mean he doesn't scare you?'

'Me?' Johnny scoffed. 'I'm not afraid of Dusty Fog. And one of these days I aim to get him and——'

Johnny allowed the words to fade off, but conveyed the impression that what he aimed to do to Dusty Fog would not be pleasant.

'How long are you in New York for?' asked Defluer, controlling a stomach which still protested at the ghastly sight he'd seen in Miller's place. He had listened to the conversation and his thoughts ran along the same lines as were Drinkwater's at this moment.

'Figured to head back west any time,' replied Johnny truthfully. He knew Miller would not easily forget or forgive him and this was Miller's range. A man ended nowhere but in a pine-wood box and laid six foot under ground by bucking that sort of game on the other side's range. So Johnny allowed to take the first west bound train, making for his own country. Then, happen Miller felt like it, Johnny stood full ready and willing to face him down.

'We're going to Texas on Monday,' Paulette put in. 'To stay on Basil's ranch. I'm so looking forward to it.'

She had shaken off much of her sick feeling by now and her cheeks slowly regained their colour as she thought of the holiday.

'Why not travel down with us,' suggested Drinkwater. 'My—er—the ranch is in Teckman County, and it borders the Rio Hondo. We might need help if the Rio Hondo crowd make trouble. I would like a good man who knows them along with me.'

Johnny opened his mouth to say something, then closed it again with the words unsaid. He had a feeling that more than just a casual request for company lay behind the offer

40

to accompany Drinkwater's party down to Texas. They didn't look the sort who would ask a stranger along without real good reason, especially a stranger who clearly didn't belong to their class of folks. He decided he might as well play along with his unexpected hosts and travel back to Texas with them.

'Why sure,' he drawled. 'I'd admire to come along with you.'

'I think it might be advisable for you to stay at my place,' Drinkwater went on. 'I'll arrange for your belongings to be collected from wherever you are staying, one of my men will pick them up in the morning. Then I'll find out if the police are taking any interest in the shooting. I doubt if they will be. By the time the police reached Miller's he would have made sure no sign of the wounded man was seen. If the police know anything I'll go along and straighten things out for you. But as I said, Miller won't want any trouble, especially shooting trouble, around his place.'

'I heard tell you folks in the big city don't cotton to folks protecting themselves,' Johnny agreed. 'This's your range, friend. I'll leave it to you how you handle things.'

They dropped Paulette off at her home before driving on to Drinkwater's house. Johnny found himself treated to a good meal, then shown to a small room upstairs. He sat on the bed for a time, thinking over the events of the evening, trying to decide what to make of Drinkwater's interest in the Rio Hondo country, and the small man's fear of trouble. Johnny decided to wait and see. He undressed and rolled into the comfortable bed.

Downstairs, in the library, Drinkwater and Defluer sat facing each other.

'Do you think he's all right?' Defluer asked.

'I think he is. But I wish Acre hadn't left town. I would have liked his opinion of Raybold.'

'I saw Raybold draw his gun and shoot,' Defluer pointed out. 'I've never seen anything so fast in all my life. And he sounded so sincere when he said he ran Dusty Fog out of that town.'

'He was with that gal and they came from Daniels' place,' Drinkwater went on. 'You know what the Lion's Den is like.'

'Even a rougher place than Miller's,' Defluer replied. 'You don't think Raybold is an outlaw, do you?'

'It's a possibility. Although I'm less interested in that than in the fact that he doesn't act scared of facing Dusty Fog. I think we should take him along with us. If he's the sort of man we want we will hire him on our arrival at the ranch.'

CHAPTER FIVE

SUE BLAZE MEETS HER KIN

Never during the one year, three months, one week and two days that they had been married could Sue Blaze recall seeing her husband act so quiet and subdued as he did this morning. Sue felt puzzled for Red had never been the sort of man who worried, or acted subdued. Yet that was just how he looked and acted as they rode the buggy along the trail to the O.D. Connected ranch house on a visit to his kin, the first since their arrival in the Rio Hondo country from Arizona.

'Now you-all stop that worrying, Red boy,' she told him. 'It won't be as bad as all that.'

Sue Blaze was small, petite and very pretty. Today she wore a sun-bonnet on her short, curly blonde hair, hair which looked almost as uncombed and unruly as her husband's most times. She also wore a neat print dress which showed a good, shapely figure to its best advantage, even though she did not like to wear such a garment and only did so on special occasions. This day came under the heading. In a short time she would be meeting the head of the Hardin, Fog and Blaze clan, the one man her husband feared more than any other in the world. Ole Devil Hardin.

'I bet he's nowhere's bad as you reckon,' Sue went on as the buggy rolled slowly up the ridge which hid the O.D. Connected house from her view.

'He sure isn't, honey,' agreed Red fervently. 'He's worse.'

'Just let him try and bully *my* Red!' thought Sue grimly. 'I'll sure tell him where he comes off.'

Yet, for all of that she felt a twinge of nervousness as they topped the ridge and she caught her first glimpse of the O.D. Connected's main ranch buildings. What she saw did not make her feel any more at ease. Sue came from a ranch, had been born and raised on one, but not such a ranch as the O.D. Connected. The whole of Backsight County in which her old home had been situated, could fit into the great ranges of the O.D. Connected.

'That's Uncle Devil out on the porch,' Red said in a tone which implied he would as soon turn the buggy and high-tail it for home as go on.

The words might have annoyed Sue, but she knew they did not come from any shame Red might feel about her. Red had the misfortune of being himself, wild, fun-loving, reckless. In this he often came into conflict with his Uncle Devil both as cowhand and cavalry officer in the Texas Light Cavalry during the war. Now Red tended to regard a visit to meet his uncle on the same level as a trip to the dentist's.

While the buggy rolled down the slope Sue took time out to study the man who sat on the porch and the girl who came from the house towards him as they topped the ridge. Her attention went mainly to the man, wishing to form her own opinion of him. He sat in the wheelchair which was his home since he tried to ride a seventeen hand paint stallion —and failed.* Around his lower body, covering his legs, hung a tartan blanket. The upper torso was clad in a white, frilly bosomed shirt with a string bow tie, and a stylish grey cutaway coat. He sat straight, square and iron-backed as a soldier riding in review before the President. His face, tanned by the sun, still looked imperious, strong, masterful, the black eyes firm and commanding. Sue saw all this and gained the impression that Ole Devil Hardin would be a born leader, yet of the kind who kept the liking and respect of his men. Being tied down in the wheelchair had neither weakened his powers, nor caused him to sink into self-pity.

Next Sue looked at the girl. She would be about Sue's height and even at that distance looked truly beautiful. It was a different kind of beauty from Sue's, more worldly perhaps. Yet the girl had an air, that undefinable something which set a lady aside no matter what she wore. Not even being clad in a tartan shirt-waist, jeans and hunting boots could hide her air of breeding and charm. Her hair was black and shiny, hanging long at the back in what would one day be known as a pony tail. Her figure, in the shirt

* Told in *The Fastest Gun in Texas*, by J. T. Edson. Wagon Wheel Western. W 231.

and jeans, looked rich, full and mature.

Neither Ole Devil Hardin nor his grand-daughter Betty noticed the buggy at first. Ole Devil laid aside his book as he heard the soft footsteps behind him and saw the four blue-tick hounds start to beat their tails on the porch floor. Betty came forward and laid a hand gently on his shoulder.

'And where are you going, young lady?'

'That cougar jumped a colt down by the Rio Hondo woods,' she replied, her voice refined, with just a gentle hint of the strength which could come into it when something annoyed her. 'With the crew out at the round-up camp somebody has to get it before it takes more.'

'Huh!' he grunted, looking her up and down. 'I spend money having you educated at a fancy dude school back east, and you run around all wild and woodsey like a tomboy.'

'I always told you it was a waste of time,' she replied with an air of triumph. 'Now you've admitted it—land-sakes, Grandfather, why didn't you say we had company calling.'

The latter words came as the blue-tick hounds lurched to their feet and left the porch raising their voices to the sky as they headed for the approaching buggy.

'Figured you'd get to know soon enough,' replied Ole Devil, not admitting he had failed to notice the buggy until this moment. 'And call off those fool hounds before they spook the horse.'

Betty laughed and called a command which brought the big hounds back to her. She then looked at the buggy and the merry glint in her eyes grew more merry as she watched Red's face.

'I bet poor Cousin Red's quaking in his boots,' she said. 'Whenever he has to come and see you he always reminds me of a little boy called out in front of the class to tell the school teacher why he was flipping peach-pips around the room.'

'Hush up, gal!' growled Ole Devil. 'You make me sound like an old ogre.'

'You act like one most times,' Betty replied and gently squeezed his arm.

By this time the buggy had halted before the house. Red sprang down and went around to help Sue alight. He took her by the arm and led her towards the porch.

'Uncle Devil, Cousin Betty,' he said, still holding Sue's arm as if afraid she might bolt, and stepping on to the porch to face his kin. 'This's my wife. Sue, I'd like to present Uncle Devil and Cousin Betty Hardin.'

'Come here, gal,' said Ole Devil gently, holding out his hands.

Sue stepped from Red's side, holding out both her hands. Suddenly she became painfully aware that her hands did not have a soft feminine whiteness. They were strong little hands which had done their fair share of hard work and this did not leave a lady-like softness.

Taking the girl's hands in his own Ole Devil held them while he looked her up and down. In that moment Sue lost all her fear of the stern-faced old man. Hard as nails he might be, iron disciplinarian he undoubtedly had been and most likely still was, but only when the occasion demanded it. Yet underneath all that lay a kindness and gentleness which she felt and warmed to.

'Red,' said Ole Devil gently, far more gently than his usual tone when addressing the young cowhand. 'You've married a charming and beautiful young lady.' A grim smile flickered across his face. 'One who should be a steadying influence on you, or I miss my guess—and not before time.'

From the way Red's chest puffed out at the words it seemed fortunate that his wife employed stout cotton to stitch the buttons on his shirt.

Then Betty and Sue faced each other and gripped each other's hands. Much to Sue's surprise Betty's hands felt strong and had done plenty of work, not at all what she expected from a rich southern belle. Betty looked Sue over, taking her measure and liking what she saw. Sue realised that she had made a friend and warmed to Betty from the start. They kissed then Betty threw a look at Red.

'Sue,' she said, but her smile and tone belied the words. 'Any girl unfortunate enough to marry one of my kin deserves my deepest sympathy. Cousin Red, you couldn't have picked a sweeter, nicer girl.'

'Draw up a chair for your lady, Red,' Ole Devil ordered. 'You're not fixing to head for home yet awhile, are you?'

'Well, no, sir,' Red replied, bringing chairs for the girls and seating Sue close to Ole Devil.

46

'Fine,' barked Ole Devil. 'Tommy!'

The last came as a yell which brought a small, Oriental man from the house. The man grinned a gold-toothed welcome at Red as he came forward. He was Tommy Okasi and had been Ole Devil's servant for more years than Red could remember, without ever appearing to age any, Red thought as he looked Tommy over.

'Red-san,' Tommy said, then bowed to Sue. 'Humble self takes pleasure in meeting wife of Red-san.'

Ole Devil threw a defiant look at Betty. 'Burgundy for two and wine for the ladies, Tommy. If Mrs. Blaze will allow her husband to toast the marriage?'

'Of course I will, sir,' Sue replied, blushing just a trifle.

Once more Red's chest swelled fit to burst his shirt buttons. Only on very rare occasions were the younger members of the clan allowed to sample Ole Devil's fine old burgundy.

'We'd've been here sooner, sir,' Red remarked, petting the hounds which came around him. 'But I stayed on to help Colonel Raines get his spread working.'

'So I gathered from the couple of letters you sent. Still writing letters or reports was never your strong suit, was it?'

'No, sir. It never was.'

The drinks arrived and Ole Devil proposed a toast to Red and Sue's marriage, expressing the hope it would be long, happy and fruitful.

'Are you staying on here, boy?' Ole Devil asked.

'We hoped to get a little spread of our own, sir,' Red replied. 'Pete's fixing to marry come spring and the Double B will be a mite crowded for us all.'

'Good idea, getting a place,' drawled Ole Devil and asked no more questions.

Sue and Red had decided to strike out on their own. Yet both felt worried about Ole Devil's reaction to the news. Now Red found that his uncle regarded him as a man, grown and full capable of handling his own affairs. Ole Devil would give any advice he could, offer any help, but would not try to influence Red's decision one way or the other.

'Now we're for it!' Betty remarked, rising, setting her wine glass on a small table and pointing across the range.

47

The others looked in the direction she pointed. A large bunch of men came riding at a gallop towards the buildings, wild cowhand yells rang out from the riders and their mounts sprang forward at a better pace.

'The round-up crew,' Ole Devil said. 'They're back earlier than I expected.'

'I was out by their camp yesterday,' Betty replied. 'Dusty told them if they finished the last gather today they'd all go to Diggers Wells and have a time. It sure got the boys working like nothing else would.'

Ole Devil nodded. He knew how the crew enjoyed a trip to Diggers Wells when their segundo, Dusty Fog, rode with them. He also knew Dusty would not allow the men to skimp their work. If Dusty brought the crew in he was fully satisfied that the full round-up had been completed correctly.

Four horses, two big paints, an equally big bloodbay and a really fine looking white swung away from the main bunch. Travelling at a dead run, ridden by men who were masters in all matters equine, the horses, not one of them standing less than seventeen hands, came towards the main house. Sue watched them, a smile on her face. She knew three of the riders, the fourth was a stranger, the boy Waco she had heard about.

At first it appeared the horses might ride straight up on the porch. A touch of the reins brought each animal to a rump-scraping halt and the riders jumped from their saddles.

Tallest of all by a good three inches stood a handsome gold-blond giant with the features and physique of a Greek god of old. His clothes might be work stained, but they were the dress of a range country dandy, yet the low hanging, matched ivory butted Colt Cavalry Peacemakers hung in the holsters of a real fast man's gun-rig and were no decoration or the signs lied badly. His name, Mark Counter.

Next to Mark stood the Ysabel Kid, six foot of lean, deadly, whang-leather tough deadliness, with a dark yet almost babyishly innocent appearing face and cold hundred-year-old red hazel eyes. A low crowned, wide brimmed black hat sat on the Kid's raven black hair. The rest of his clothing, bandana, shirt, levis, boots, all were black. Even his gunbelt had been tooled in black leather. Only the walnut grips of the old Colt Dragoon revolver hanging butt forward at his right side and the ivory hilt of the bowie knife at his left served to change the blackness.

Waco, the young man Sue did not yet know, stood in height between Mark and the Kid. A blond haired, wide shouldered, lean waisted young man in his late teens. His range clothes had the look of a tophand about them, despite his youth. The matched staghorn butted Colt Artillery Peacemakers resting their five and a half inch barrels in his holsters also told a tale, happen a man knew what to look for. They hung just right, in the manner of one who was real good with his guns. This handsome youngster might not have reached his twentieth birthday yet, but he stood a man full-grown in western eyes.

The last of the quartet was Dusty Fog, Confederate Civil War hero. The man whose Colt guns took the first prize in the match at Cochise County Fair. The man Aristes Defluer claimed shot his son in the back and laughed as he did so.

Yet Dusty Fog's hair was a dusty blond colour. He needed a shave but under no circumstances could the three day growth be called a beard. His face had been tanned by the elements. It was a handsome face, strong, self-reliant, intelligent and in no way brutal or the sort of face described by Defluer's witness. His shoulders were wide and hinted at strength, yet he did not show it as did Mark Counter. The clothes Dusty wore had cost as much as Mark's, were not so eye-catching, nor did Dusty set them off so well. Around his waist hung a gunbelt with a brace of bone handled Colt Civilian Peacemakers, butt forward for a cross draw, in the holsters. In a way the guns looked out of place on such a man, yet nobody who saw them come into Dusty's hands and roar ever thought that way again.

This then was Dusty Fog. Only he differed from the description Defluer heard in several vital details. The main being that he was no burly giant, not unless the witness lived in a land where five foot six in height be regarded as gigantic. For Dusty Fog stood only five foot six.

'Sue honey!' Mark Counter greeted, coming forward. 'I just knew you'd come back to me.'

'You?' gasped Sue. 'I've enough with one worthless man,

without taking on a big ox like you.'

'That's telling him, Sue,' Betty put in. 'You'll have to watch Red now this worthless bunch are back.'

'I've got him house-broke now,' Sue replied. 'It's all done by kindness and the bottom of a skillet when he gets uppy.'

Ole Devil threw a glance at his grand-daughter. 'Now Red's married and settled down it's time I thought about getting you off my hands. How about it, Mark?'

'About what, sir?'

'Betty'd make a right becoming wife, don't you reckon?'

'She sure would, sir,' agreed Mark. 'Happen I hear tell of anyone who wants one I'll let you know.'

Betty looked ready to explode as her grandfather glanced at the Kid.

'You, Lon?'

'I'd sure admire to marry her. Only us Comanches have to bring hosses for a bride price. I'll just head out and catch some. Be back right smart in five or ten years and marry her like a shot.'

'Which same I'm too young, sweet and innocent to take up a wife, or I'd take her off your hands, sir,' Waco drawled, before he could be asked.

'Grandpappy!' Betty gasped. 'Do you mean you'd marry me to one of this idle, shiftless, worthless bunch?'

'No such luck,' grunted Ole Devil. 'Wouldn't say they've too much sense, but they can run too fast for that.'

Dusty Fog did not follow the rest to the porch. He opened his saddle-bag and lifted out the tally book. The other cowhands drew to one side, to introduce Waco and talk over old times. This left Ole Devil free to discuss serious ranch business with his segundo.

'We made a good gathering, sir,' Dusty told the old man. 'Our herds are coming up to expectation. Found a couple hundred head of old Johnson's Lazy J stock. I thought to leave word in Diggers for the new folks at the spread to collect them if they want them. I didn't know Cousin Red was back or we wouldn't have fixed to go in to Diggers with the boys.'

At that moment Sue came over.

'Waco says you're headed for Diggers Wells, Dusty,' she said.

'Were, we'll stop here now.'

'Not if I can help it,' she snorted, knowing how a ranch crew enjoyed a trip to town with their boss along. 'Do you think I want you and that wild bunch underfoot while I'm getting to know Uncle Devil? I have enough trouble with that worthless Red of mine without you.'

Dusty and Ole Devil exchanged grins. 'I don't know if all females are that ornery,' Dusty drawled, 'or if it's knowing Cousin Betty gets them that way. Hey, Red, you-all riding into Diggers with us?'

'Me?' asked Red, looking horrified at the thought. 'As if I'd go to a place like Diggers.'

'That's right as the off side of a hoss, boy,' Sue replied. 'You sure won't!'

Turning to Betty, Dusty said, 'Will you tend to paying the crew for me? I want to take a bath and change before I ride.'

'I'll do it. Looks like I won't get out after that old cougar today anyhow and so I may as well get you crowd off the place as quick as I can.'

Two hours later Red Blaze stood on the porch and watched the O.D. Connected crew, all washed, shaved and changed into their go-to-town low-necked clothes and on their favourite horses, ride out on a spree to Diggers Wells. He thought back on the days when he would have been part of such a gathering, the wildest of them all and the one most bent on enjoying himself to the full.

A hand slipped under his arm and he looked down into his wife's eyes. Sue must have been able to read his thoughts for she asked:

'You know you could have gone if you wanted, don't you?'

'Reckon I do, honey. Only it wouldn't be the same.'

'You—you don't regret marrying me?'

Red scooped her into his arms and kissed her, then pushed her back to arm's length and looked straight into her face.

'Know something, Mrs. Susan Theodore Blaze?' he asked. 'I only ever did one real smart thing in my life. That was marrying you.'

CHAPTER SIX

DIGGERS WELLS

There'd be about two more hours of daylight before the sun set and night fell on the town of Diggers Wells.

On a bench at the end of town sat two leathery old-timers, men who had been in Diggers Wells ever since the first hut rose from the prairie grass. They each held a stick and whittled at it with the quiet attention of idlers performing a pleasant and unrewarding task. Then one threw a glance along the trail which led to the Rio Hondo.

'They're coming!' he said in apparent satisfaction.

His friend raised a pair of sun-squinted eyes and studied the dust cloud, judged its implications with the ease of one who learned to tell the size of a Comanche raiding party by the dust it stirred up.

'More than just the O.D. Connected,' he stated.

'Huh huh!'

'Be stirring times in town tonight. One way or another.'

They whittled on for a time, but their mind clearly was no longer on the task. The man who spoke first eased himself more comfortably.

'Gallom ain't going to like it.'

'Gallom's a Kansas lawman. He'll stay away from those Rio Hondo boys, especially if that there paint in the lead's rid by who we know's riding it.'

'Two paints, Sam,' corrected his friend.

Sam Chord grunted. His eyes were no less keen than in the days when he rode with the Texas Light Cavalry against the Mexican Rancheros and Lancers.

'Yeah, feller at the right's too tall for Cap'n Fog. Be the boy, Waco, or whichever he calls hisself.'

Nearer thundered the horses. Wild cowhand yells filled the air, the occasional shot cracked out. Heads popped out of windows, or peered through doors. Faces which had

52

been looking bored took on interested expressions. No longer did the town lie sleepy and dormant. Suddenly it started to throb with life as cowhands came to town.

Startled, though not frightened, dudes stared from the sidewalks, or came from the two stores. This gave the cowhands the encouragement they needed, for a cowhand was by nature an exhibitionist. They treated the dudes to a display of riding skill seldom equalled and never bettered by the performers in a Bill-show, one of the Wild West spectacles Buffalo Bill Cody and his like took east of the Mississippi for the entertainment of dudes.

Mark Counter brought his huge bloodbay stallion to a halt before a pair of pretty young eastern ladies who kept their fans raised and studied him with fluttering eye-lashes. He made a fine figure as always, one which would catch the eye in any crowd. To the girls this was the west they came to see, he looked like the kind of man they read of in the lurid little blood-and-thunder books of the period and made a change from the hands at the ranch. Unfortunately, before any conversation could ensue, their mother appeared and escorted them hurriedly back into the store once more.

With a grin Mark turned his horse and headed for the saloon where the rest of the party were dismounting and looking for space to tether their horses.

This proved to be something of a problem for the O.D. Connected crew met up with the Double B boys, led by their bosses Buck and Pete Blaze, also headed for town with the expressed intention of showing the fancy dude gals from the Lazy J what they didn't necessarily have to go on missing.

Buck and Pete Blaze looked slightly older, not so fiery-haired or reckless versions of Red. They were twins and so much alike that only Red could tell them apart. So, unless they aimed to have a joke on with somebody, the two brothers dressed in different coloured clothes. They were with Dusty at the hitching rail, securing their horses.

'The great siezer's coming, Dusty,' Buck remarked, nodding towards the town jail.

Turning, Dusty looked along the street. Three men came towards them, three men wearing law badges and carrying ten gauge shotguns. Only one of the trio was of any interest to Dusty. The other two were just cheap, hired hard-cases.

Their kind infested every trail end town, ready to do anything but work and willing to back any play if the money should be good and the risks not too great. Sure they were dangerous happen a dozen or so of them came on a man when he was drunk and unable to defend himself. To a sober man who could handle himself their kind meant less than nothing.

The other man might be dangerous. He stood six foot tall, had heavy shoulders encased in a stylish black cutaway jacket. His shirt, tie and fancy vest had the style of a gambling man while his trousers and town boots never saw a day's hard range work. That low hanging Colt looked like it had been used some and he handled his shotgun in the manner of one who knew what it was for. On his vest glinted the badge of the great siezer, the town marshal.

'Name's Gallom, Dusty. Gus Gallom,' drawled Buck. 'One of the Earp fighting pimps from Dodge City. The dude spread brought him in a month back to make sure us wild cowhands didn't horraw their visitors any.'

'Best go see what he wants then,' Dusty replied.

With that he swung away from his horse, Buck at his heels. The other members of the two ranch crews stood on the sidewalk and waited to see what Gallom, who, the prairie telegraph had it, claimed he aimed to keep the cowhands under control in his town, said to their bosses.

Gallom halted in the centre of the street, his two men swinging out on either flank, although neither showed any great enthusiasm when they saw the group of cowhands on the sidewalk and the two men who came towards them. Buck Blaze had a name for being a ringtailed ripper in his own right and, while they did not know him, they could tell that Dusty stood as one of the real good men with guns.

In this the gun-hand deputies showed more knowledge than their boss. Gallom threw a glance at Dusty and wondered why so small and insignificant a man stepped out to represent his spread. Gallom's lips curled in a sneer. Happen that runt was trying to act big he could soon be cut down to size.

'You bossing this lot?' Gallom asked.

'Reckon,' drawled Buck. 'You'll be the new marshal?'

'I am. The name's Gus Gallom.'

'I'm Buck Blaze from the Double B,' Buck introduced. 'This here's my cousin, Dusty Fog.'

For a long moment Gallom did not reply to this. He threw a glance at the two men siding him, hoping to see a sneer of disbelief on each face. Cold realisation slugged him in the stomach with the power of a mule-kick. His men did not doubt that Buck Blaze spoke the truth. This small man really was the Rio Hondo gun wizard Dusty Fog.

'You wanted to see us, Mr. Gallom?' asked Dusty.

Which showed Gallom right where he stood in Dusty's eyes. No Texan used the word 'mister' if he knew the other man's christian name—unless he wanted it known he did not like the man.

'I came to tell you this section's got a lot of eastern folks staying here. We don't figure on having them scared by wild riding cowhands trying to tree the town.'

'Who don't?' asked Buck.

'The folks who hired me.'

'And who might they be?' Dusty inquired.

'The citizens of Diggers Wells!' growled Gallom, bluster in his voice.

'Do tell,' Dusty drawled. 'Now listen good to me, Mr. Gallom. We've been coming in to Diggers Wells for more years than I can remember and I've never known the folks to object to us.'

'I'm warning y——'

'No, mister!' Dusty interrupted, his voice as cold and gentle as the first warning whisper of a Texas blue norther storm. 'I'm *telling* you. When old Sam Chord or any of the other folks from town come up and tell me they don't want O.D. Connected or Double B here, then I'll listen. But not to you, or your boss at that fancy dude spread. I'll keep the boys in reasonable bounds. They won't rough up your folks or molest their women. But happen those dudes or yours don't care for our company they've a real answer—stay out of town until we've gone.'

Which laid down the matter as plain as a Texas boy could lay it before a Kansas lawman. Now it all rested on the way Gus Gallom aimed to take things. The chips lay on the table, the last card dealt and he could call the bet, or throw in his hand. He threw a glance at the cowhands before the saloon. In his time Gallom had seen the big crews, Shanghai Pierce's, Clay Allison's, Charlie Goodnight's, hard bunches all. But the men before Big Ethel's saloon were just as hard, tough and salty as the best.

Suddenly, to Gallom's eyes, Dusty Fog no longer looked small. Now he seemed to stand taller than any other man on the street. Gallom could try and fool himself that he backed down because of overwhelming numbers, but in his heart he knew it to be a lie. He backed down from Dusty Fog.

'I'll bear it in mind!' Gallom spat out, the words coming bitter as bile. He was backing down, singing low like so many other Kansas lawmen sung low in the presence of the small Texan known as Dusty Fog.

'Happen any of our boys get out of line and you jail them,' Dusty carried on, 'I'll want to see them unmarked in the morning—understand?'

'Yeah. I understand.'

More than one Texas boy had been hauled into a Kansas jail and worked over by the deputies. Gallom in his time had helped use the boot, or a leather belt, on some of them. He knew one thing for sure, any man of either crew he picked up would be kept in a cell and would not be marked.

'Just as long as you do,' drawled Dusty. 'Let's go, Cousin Buck.'

Gallom turned, snarling out a low curse which, fortunately, did not reach Dusty's ears. The marshal walked back in the direction of the jail, followed by his relieved looking deputies. Gallom thought of the plans he had made on being brought in to Diggers Wells. He saw the possibilities of owning a saloon and gambling house in the town. The dudes from the Lazy J came to town with money in their pockets, money to spend—or lose on gambling tables in which the house did no gambling but stood certain to win all the time. Already he had started his plans to drive Big Ethel first out of business, then out of town. Then he would put his own people in to start operations. He saw how he might be able to use the incident of the cowhand influx to move in on her. In the morning, with the ranch crews back at their own spreads he would show Big Ethel and the town of Diggers Wells who really ran things.

Not knowing what thoughts Gallom harboured the Texans fell back to allow their bosses lead the way into Big Ethel's place. Inside Dusty Fog came to a halt, looking around him in some surprise. Usually, especially when the crews came into town, the saloon would be jumping with life, band playing, girls waiting to entertain the hands, gambling tables inviting all and sundry to chance their luck at licking the house percentage. Mostly Big Ethel herself looked like the happiest woman alive, her booming laughter sounding all over the building. When Big Ethel neither laughed nor smiled things were bad indeed.

Something of the old Big Ethel welcome came to her face and died again. The Texas men crowded forward and Mark Counter gripped her around her ample waist, then hoisted her six foot of bulky heft on to the bar top with little more effort than if she weighed no more than a baby.

'What's wrong in here, Ethel honey?' he asked. 'You holding a wake?'

'Where-at's the gals, Ethel?' said the Ysabel Kid.

'Upstairs, Lon.'

'Then you-all get them down here and give us some music!' ordered the Kid. 'I been chasing cows for over a month and I want a change.'

Big Ethel shook her head. 'I can't do it, Lon. Gallom's said there'll be no music, gals or gambling in here. He'll close me down if I go against his words.'

'Ethel gal,' drawled the Kid, 'you got no say in it at all.'

Turning, the Kid looked towards where Ethel's musicians sat at their table. Until the arrival of the cowhands a desultory game of stud poker had been in progress but now the men sat waiting developments. They saw the Kid's face take on an innocent expression all knew too well. When the Ysabel Kid got to looking as innocent as a church pew of choirboys it behoved all around to sit well back and watch him with both eyes.

'Gents,' he said, and though his voice sounded mild the musicians conjured up pictures of Comanche Dog Soldiers out hunting for white scalps, 'you-all got the count of five to be up there on the bandstand and playing "Ole Dan Tucker". One!'

A good three before the Kid reached his five count the

orchestra had hit the stage, grabbed their instruments and started to produce the stirring notes of the old song he requested.

High heeled boots thudded on planking, Kelly spurs jingled and voices lifted in speech or laughter. From the upstairs rooms Big Ethel's girls peered forth, saw who stood inside the big bar-room and knew they could safely come down. Gallom would never dare show his face inside the room while the O.D. Connected and Double B celebrated within.

For the first time, as the gambling tables uncovered and all the normal sounds rang out, Mark took a good look at the tall, black haired woman called Big Ethel. He gave a low growl and reached a hand to turn her left cheek towards him. Under the make-up showed a dull bruise.

'Who did it, Ethel?' he asked.

She did not reply immediately, knowing what would be the outcome if she spoke. Mark would not be put off however.

'Was it that loud-mouthed Yankee mac who's got himself elected town law?' he went on.

Big Ethel nodded, knowing Mark would likely find out one way or another. She also knew that mac used in such a manner had no connection with Scotland. It meant a pimp and was the label Texas men tied to most law enforcement officers who hailed from, or served, the Territory of Kansas. Ethel shot out a hand to catch Mark's arm as he turned, feeling the giant muscles under the shirt.

'Leave it lie, Mark!' she said urgently. 'Please, for my sake.'

'Wouldn't take me but a couple of minutes at most,' he answered.

'No, Mark. He's been hired by that Lazy J bunch. They've got big money behind them, more than I want to buck. Just let it ride, word has it the big boss is due out here soon. When he comes I'll put things up to him and see how he stands. But I have to be clean to do it. How'll it look if he hears one of my friends roughed up and run out the feller he brought in as law.'

'Man should know better than hire Kansas law into Texas,' replied Mark.

'Happen you went to New York would you know their

58

ways?' she countered. 'Let it ride, Mark—for me.'

Mark smiled and relaxed. He could see Big Ethel's point. 'I'll do it, Ethel gal. Just for you. But don't let Dusty see that bruise or he's likely to go down to the jail and take Gallom apart with his bare hands.'

CHAPTER SEVEN

THE END OF A KANSAS LAWMAN

'Now that was what I call a night, Whitey!'

Big Ethel spoke expansively as she looked around her saloon in the cold grey light of dawn, or as near the cold grey light of dawn as nine o'clock in the morning could be.

Following the usual procedure Big Ethel and Whitey were in the empty and deserted bar-room checking up on damage done by the previous night's celebrations and on the stock situation. True the O.D. Connected and Double B weren't likely to be back in full strength, but a few of them would be coming in. The local spreads were near to finishing their round-ups now, soon they ought to be streaming into town and it would not pay to be short of anything the cowhands wanted.

Things had been so near back to the good old days the previous evening that Big Ethel had just about forgotten the menace of Gus Gallom and his threats of closure if she went against his word.

She remembered Gallom again—real quick.

The batwing doors burst open. Big Ethel turned, the colour drained from her unpainted cheeks, the bruise left by Gallom's hand showing plainly against the pallor of her skin.

Gallom stood at the door, behind him four of his deputies, each holding a heavy axe. Beyond them, through the door, Big Ethel could see the other two deputies facing and holding back the crowd of curious citizens who gathered to discover what brought their unwanted town marshal to Big Ethel's place at this hour of the morning and on what clearly looked like a clean-up session.

There was hate and worse in Gallom's eyes as he started forward across the floor, the four deputies following, grinning at the thought of an orgy of wrecking with free drinks thrown in.

'What do you want, Gallom?' Big Ethel asked, although she knew without needing to speak.

'Mr. Gallom to you!' he answered, the snarl in his voice sounding wolf-savage. 'You know what I'm here for. You went against my word. I said you didn't have music, your painted whores and crooked gambling going.'

'There's no whores or crooked gambling in here, Gallom, and well you know it,' Big Ethel snapped, loyalty to her girls over-riding her fear. 'But there soon would be if I took you in as a partner.'

He lashed around a backhand slap which staggered Big Ethel back into the bar, blood trickling from the corner of her mouth. Whitey came over the bar top like a catch-dog after a cougar, throwing himself at the bigger man. With a grin one of the deputies lashed his axe around, the blunt end crashing into Whitey's middle. The little man folded over and Gallom's knee drove up, smashing into the doubled-over face. Whitey came erect, went backwards to crash into the bar at his boss's side, then slowly slide to the floor.

Big Ethel lost her temper then. She saw Gallom coming at her and threw a clenched-fist punch which smashed into his face, sprawling him backwards. The woman knew how to throw a punch and carried some weight and strength behind her shoulder. Gallom crashed into a chair, exploding it under him as he went to the floor.

One of the deputies let his axe fall and drove a brutal fist into Big Ethel's stomach. She gave a croaking gasp and collapsed to the floor, moaning and trying to gasp air into her lungs.

Spitting blood and curses Gallom made his feet. He strode forward and drove a kick into Big Ethel's ribs. The woman saw it coming and tried to roll clear. She missed the full rib-breaking force of the kick, but it still hurt and she stayed down, unable to shake off the pain sufficiently to allow herself any chance of self-protection.

Gallom dug his fingers into Big Ethel's hair and hauled her to her feet by it. His eyes glowed with madness almost as he caught her by the wrist. One twist took the wrist up Big Ethel's back, held there and sending waves of pain beating through her.

'You and those damned Texans made a fool of me!' he snarled in Big Ethel's ear. 'I'll show you! I'm taking you outside there and you're going to tell the folks you're a lousy madam, you run a whore house and you cheated those folks from the spread last night. And my deputies are going to wreck your place, then I'll slip a padlock on it and run you out of town.'

The sick aching pain which ran through her body prevented Ethel from making any reply. She gave a moan as Gallom applied more pressure to her arm. Then Gallom started walking her across the floor to the batwing doors. He paused and looked to his men.

'Make it look good!' he ordered. 'Only don't touch the gambling tables and the bar. We'll need them ourselves.'

A growl of objection and anger rolled up from the growing crowd of citizens. Even the women in Diggers Wells liked and respected Big Ethel. Their anger rolled up and the menfolk scowled, wondering how they ever come to allow Gallom to take over as their marshal. The two deputies at the door hefted their shotguns and moved to the edge of the sidewalk ready to give their moral support.

'All right!' Gallom snarled, forcing Big Ethel from the sidewalk and on to the street. He twisted her arm again and brought another moan from her. 'You're going to tell these folks just what you are. Then they'll not be so all-fired keen to let you stay on here.'

In this Gallom followed a time-honoured Kansas lawman procedure. He wanted to give the crowd an excuse to overlook his actions. Later, when he ran the saloon, he could win the local folks over with judicious donations to public funds. Only he wanted to establish Big Ethel's guilt, even though that guilt be manufactured, to salve consciences later.

Big Ethel gritted her teeth, biting down another moan and saying nothing. She felt Gallom give her arm another savage twisting jolt. Pain lined her face and brought tears to her eyes. Through them she saw an old man, old Sam Chord, step out of the crowd and tried to warn him to stand back.

'Let her go, Gallom!' snapped the old man.

In his time Sam Chord rode for the Texas Light Cavalry

and as a scout in the Indian wars. His old Navy Colt hung in an open topped holster and he knew how to handle it. The two deputies tensed, then relaxed again. The crowd looked ready to take cards and a man could not buck such odds—not and leave the field any other way than feet first.

Hidden behind Big Ethel's bulk Gallom released her wrist with one hand, lowered it and lifted clear his Colt, keeping the gun out of sight. He snarled over Big Ethel's shoulder, spitting out the words at Chord:

'Get out of it, you old goat!'

Chord ignored the warning and stepped forward. 'I said leave her be!'

The gun came into sight and roared. Sam Chord jerked as lead struck him. He reeled back a couple of steps and fell to the ground, his gun still in its holster. The crowd's combined voice rose in an angry snarl. The deputies hefted their shotguns for they knew it would be fight or wind up doing a cottonwood hoedown. Gallom had gone way too far when he shot down the old man in cold blood.

'Lousy murdering skunk, Gallom!' said Chord's old whittling partner in a rage and grief filled voice. 'I'll see you hang for this.'

'Yeah?' snarled Gallom, fear, hate and menace mingling in his tones. 'You'll have to take me first.'

'I can do that, too!'

The voice did not come from the crowd, but from the corner of Big Ethel's saloon. It brought every eye, including Gallom's, to the speaker and caused the menacing crowd to back off out of range of bullets which all knew would soon by flying.

Gallom felt a sudden panic bite into him. The voice came from his left side and he turned his head, knowing full well who stood there. So did his deputies for they let the muzzles of their shotguns sink towards the ground.

Standing at the corner, his *amigos* in a loose half-circle behind him, each stood so he could see and throw lead, was Dusty Fog. He, Mark, the Ysabel Kid and Waco faced Gallom, the marshal read his fate in their faces.

This was not the Dusty Fog who celebrated in Big Ethel's saloon the previous night. Gone was the friendly, cheery air. In its place stood Dusty Fog, the man who tamed Quiet Town, whose guns wrote finish to more than one aspiring fast-draw killer. He stood now as Dusty Fog the Rio Hondo gun-wizard. He stood like death with a matched brace of bone-handled Peacemaker Colts instead of a scythe.

Gallom weighed up his chances, keeping himself concealed behind Big Ethel, hiding the gun he held in his hand. He started to inch around, swinging the big woman so she acted as a shield between himself and Dusty Fog.

A crash from inside the saloon brought all attention to it. Dusty never took his eyes from Gallom as he snapped: 'Mark, Lon, Waco. In there!'

Without waiting for more instructions, or even to learn why they should go, the three men ran along the sidewalk and into the bar-room. That left Dusty standing alone against Gallom and his deputies—only the deputies knew who they were dealing with and didn't aim to take cards. A yell from inside the saloon, then the thud of a blow.

Big Ethel knew the danger to Dusty. She had shaken off most of the effects of the blow and kick, pain having cleared her head. Suddenly she twisted and heaved. The pain in her arm made her cry out and drop to her knees, but her strength and the surprise of the move got her free. Gallom stood in the open, his gun-filled hand exposed to Dusty Fog.

An almost beast-like snarl came to Gallom's lips. He died with it still there. The instant Dusty saw the gun his hands crossed, going to the butts of his twin Colts. Half a second later, while Gallom's Colt still swung towards him, Dusty threw lead. In that flickering half second, even before Gallom's drawn gun could line on Dusty and fire, he had pulled his Colts and planted a .45 bullet between Gallom's eyes. The big man's body rocked under the impact of lead, then crumpled in a heap to the ground.

There had been no other choice for Dusty but to shoot for an instant kill. He sent his lead to the one spot which would ensure Gallom could not bring the Colt into line and throw lead into him. How well he shot showed as Gallom's body sprawled in the wheel-rutted dirt of Diggers Wells' Main Street.

Not one of the crowd moved for an instant. The two deputies stood without offering to raise their weapons, clearly wondering if they were due to wind up sitting a horse under the branch of a cottonwood tree, with the hairy feel of a manilla rope around their necks. Less likely things happened in the raw western townships, especially when dealing with an enraged mob like this.

Ignoring the thuds, yells and crashes which came from inside the saloon, Dusty stepped towards the two men.

'I'll be along to the jailhouse in fifteen minutes,' he said quietly. 'I don't want to find you there.'

Which was all either man needed to hear. They turned and headed along the street at something nearer a run than a walk. Fifteen minutes they had to shake the dust of Diggers Wells from their feet. Both men allowed to be gone well within the time limit.

Dusty ignored the deputies, they would do nothing. His eyes went to where men bent over old Sam Chord's body. It was a pity about Sam, a good man. Dusty might have blamed himself for not coming sooner but he knew it to be untrue. Sam died the way he'd want to go, trying to help a friend.

'How is it, Ethel?' asked Dusty turning his attention to the big woman.

'I'll be all right,' she replied, then winced as she heard the sounds of a fight inside the saloon. 'What's happening inside?'

In the saloon Mark Counter backhanded a bloody-faced deputy over a table. In the same move he threw a punch at the second deputy, sprawling the man head over heels against the wall. Waco was ripping home punches into a third, the fourth sat against the wall, eyes glassy and mouth dropped open to show broken teeth.

Seated on the bar, legs dangling like a schoolkid at a fishing hole, the Ysabel Kid watched everything. Their entrance prevented the deputies doing more than swill some of Big Ethel's liquor and sink an axe into the top of one table. It had been the work of a moment to get the axes behind the bar, then Mark decided to show Gallom's men where they came off. In this he had Waco's support and weapons piled on the bar top. After that they set to it with a will.

To the Kid's Comanche-trained eyes fist fighting was a comparatively harmless and somewhat foolish way of settling an argument, having none of the satisfying finality of knife, war-lance or firearm. However his *amigos* liked to handle things in such a manner and the Kid did not class himself as spoilsport enough to interfere with their simple pleasures.

So, after helping the groaning Whitey to safety behind the bar, the Kid sat back and watched Mark and Waco demonstrate the noble art of bar-room brawling. In this Waco proved to have been a most apt pupil and Mark a very good teacher for the two Texans did considerable damage to the deputies.

Waco ripped a punch into the man's belly, folded him, then rose to his tip-toes with the force he threw behind the second blow. The man straightened out, spun around and went head-first through the door, shooting off the sidewalk and trying to plough a furrow in Main Street, only the hard-packed dirt of the road proved to be harder than his jaw.

Only one deputy remained on his feet. Unfortunately for him, Whitey had recovered enough to know he had been the one who struck down Big Ethel. Nor did Whitey keep this knowledge to himself.

'Me, you or both of us, Mark?' asked Waco, eyeing the deputy grimly.

They started towards the man. Fear came to his eyes and he backed towards the batwing door. Right into Dusty's arms and Dusty had heard Whitey's yelled comment on the man's actions.

Dusty caught the deputy's arm, turned him and swung a punch with the click of two king-sized billiard balls coming together. From the way the man shot sideways into the door jamb Dusty packed a considerable amount of power behind his hand when he threw a punch. The deputy let out a moaning sigh and sank to the ground.

'Did they do any damage?' gasped Big Ethel, pushing away from her helpers and making for the saloon.

'Not as much as we did last night,' Mark answered, standing by Dusty and working his fingers to take the stiffness out of them. 'We got here just in time, Dusty.'

'A mite too late,' replied Dusty, throwing a glance to where men were lifting Sam Chord's body to take it to the undertaker's. 'Get this trash on their feet and see them on their way, Mark. Some of you men take Gallom down to the undertaker's. Couple of you ladies help Big Ethel.'

Nobody thought to question his right to give orders. The women helped Big Ethel into the saloon for her ribs ached and would need tending to. The room looked little different from when Ethel left. One table was broken by the fight, another bore the mark of an axe, a few chairs went under during Mark and Waco's strenuous handling of the deputies, but no serious or permanent damage had been done.

'You all right, Boss?' Whitey asked, coming forward.

'I don't think anything's broken,' she replied. 'How about you?'

'I felt better every time Mark or Waco hit one of 'em.'

'Now you let the doctor take a look at you, Ethel,' drawled Dusty as she sank into a chair with a low groan.

'I'll do just that,' she promised, feeling at her ribs. 'Must be getting old, Dusty. Can't take it like I used to.' She threw a glance to where the Kid helped Mark and Waco to haul the moaning deputies from the building. 'How come you got here so early this morning?'

'We never left,' Dusty replied. 'Bedded down at the livery barn after we saw the boys off. I reckoned Gallom might pull something. Ought to have been on hand earlier.'

Waco stepped into the room and jerked a thumb over his shoulder. Dusty knew the sign and left Ethel to join his young friend.

'Mark sent me in, Dusty. Folks are some heated up out there, aim to head along to the Lazy J office and run the agent out of town on a rail.'

Dusty wasted no time in getting out of the room. All too well he knew the temper of a western crowd, how easy it was for some hot-head fool to yell for a rope and start a lynching party. Only fast and effective action taken early could stop such a situation and Dusty intended to see it stopped.

'Hold it!' he barked, bringing the hostile crowd swinging around to face him. 'Just where do you reckon you're going!'

'To show them fancy dudes where they come off,' replied a man Dusty knew was a loud-mouthed trouble-causer. 'They ain't bringing hired killers into this town and killing off our folks. Sam Chord's dead——'

'And the man who killed him's down at the undertaker's

by Sam's side,' Dusty replied. 'Do any of you have proof that Lazy J put him up to rough-handling Ethel!'

'They took him on!' growled the man.

'And you stood by and let him! Did any of you step up there and tell that dude agent what sort of law he hired?'

'You siding with Lazy J, Cap'n?' asked the man.

'Don't call sides on me!' Dusty snapped. 'Or I'll ram them down your neck on the heel of a Justin boot. So Gallom was a bad choice for a marshal. None of you took time out to tell that agent so. You just sat back here and let things ride on. Now you're looking to lay blame for something you could have stopped.'

A mutter rose from the crowd. They all knew every word Dusty said came out gospel-true. Not one of them had offered any kind of help or advice to the eastern man who acted as town agent for the Lazy J. Maybe the death of Sam Chord lay at their door, maybe they could have averted the killing had they spoken.

'We don't like what happened to old Sam!' said a man at the back of the crowd.

'Neither do I,' Dusty replied. 'But tearing down the Lazy J's town office won't do any good. You've seen these dudes come to town. None of them made fuss for you. They spent good money and there'll be more of them coming. That place's being run as a vacation spot for rich eastern folks and about the only place around here that they'll have to spend money is Diggers Wells. That money'll be coming to you, to the stores, the business houses. So happen you object to making money go ahead and bust the Lazy J office. Run the agent out of town on a rail if it'll make you feel any better. The folks running the Lazy J can soon enough sell up and open in another area, near some other town that the folks act friendly in. Think on it and don't come whining to me if you make the wrong decision.'

He put up one argument every member of the crowd could understand. Most of the folks ran some kind of business and had either taken profit from the dudes, or could see how they might in the near future. All remembered hearing that the Lazy J expected to house sixty or seventy guests and hoped to keep filled up all year round. That would mean steady, constant flow of money into town, far in excess of what the local ranches and the occasional visits of the Rio Hondo boys brought in.

'I'm going down to have a talk with that agent *hombre* now,' Dusty went on. 'But let me hand out some more advice. Play fair with the dudes. Don't treat them like the Kansas folks used to treat trail-drive crews. That way you'll make a steady profit and it'll last longer. And don't try to cut the cowhands out of town either. That way you'll only buy grief for yourselves and the dudes.'

With that Dusty walked away, after his friends who had been dumping the moaning deputies in the horse trough.

At the Lazy J's office Dusty rapped on the door. A voice called on him to enter so he lifted the latch and stepped in through the opening door.

Seated at his deak Frank Gurd looked at the four men who entered. He felt scared for they were the men Gallom pointed out to him on the previous day as being the leaders of the Rio Hondo crowd. They must have stayed on in town after the others left and might have something to do with the shots he had heard. He had seen Gallom that morning and heard the town marshal planned to close Big Ethel's place. The shots must mean that the attempted closure failed.

'Are you the agent for the Lazy J?' asked Dusty.

'Sure am,' Gurd replied, trying to keep his usual jovial tones.

He was a big, fat, cheery looking man, with the sort of face one trusted on sight. His face made plenty of money in the days before he took this agent job for Drinkwater, for Gurd had been a seller of gold-bricks and dud stocks or bonds.

'I just killed Gus Gallom.'

Dusty said it in a plain, matter-of-fact sort of voice which showed neither sadistic pleasure, nor remorse and guilt at having taken another man's life. He stated the plain facts, no more, no less.

Slowly Gurd sank deeper into his chair staring at the small, insignificant man before him. In his time Gurd had associated with crooks of many kinds. Yet never had he heard such a flat statement as the one uttered by Dusty.

'Y-you killed Gallom?' croaked Gurd.

'For shooting down an old man,' Dusty agreed. 'And for what he did to a lady.'

'A lady?'

'A lady, *hombre*,' growled the Kid, slit-eyed and menacing as a she-cougar cornered with a litter of new-born kittens. 'Big Ethel's played the lady every time it's been needed.'

'He told me Big Ethel was robbing our guests,' Gurd answered, not meeting any of the cold eyes. 'That he aimed to close her down. He didn't say he was going to kill anybody.'

'It maybe slipped his mind,' Mark growled.

'Mister,' Dusty cut in. 'I've got some advice that you'd better listen to and take. First, Big Ethel runs a good, clean place and the folks who came in there yesterday had fun, left after it, maybe some of them were carried to the wagon but it was real liquor and not the little green bottle under the bar that did it. Second, don't bring any more of that Kansas scum down here to handle the law. Jack Packard's county sheriff and he's got good deputies who know cowhands. If you need law get him to supply it.'

'The folks out at the ranch——!' began Gurd.

'Mister, your folks out there can come to Texas, play at being cowhands, or do whatever they want to do until hell freezes for all of me. But there's other folks use Diggers Wells and they've got to be respected same as your paying guests. Cowhands use this town, have been using it ever since the first house went up. You don't try and stop that or you'll see more trouble than a dozen lawmen can handle. Your folks acted decent enough last night, and had a good time. They can keep on having it, but the cowhands have to be given their fun too. Understand?'

'I understand.'

'Are you the big augur?' Dusty went on, then saw the other man did not understand the term. 'The boss?'

'Only the agent,' Gurd replied. He waved a hand to the two doors leading from the rear of his office. 'I stay here in town to welcome the visitors, see to them on arrival and departure, and when they come to town on a visit.' He did not mention that the big boss would arrive on the afternoon stage.

'Your boss out at the Lazy J?'

'Only the manager. The place is backed by eastern money.'

70

'You see the backers get my word,' drawled Dusty. 'Folks hereabouts are more'n a mite riled, through you bringing Gallom in and what happened this morning. One more fool mistake like that and your guests are likely to see a real old Texas custom. It's called riding a man out of town on a rail—and mister, you'll be the man doing the riding.'

'I'll remember,' Gurd replied.

'See you do!' Dusty warned and turned to walk out of the door.

Mark and the Kid followed but Waco stayed for a moment, facing the fat dude and studying him.

'Mister,' he said quietly. 'Dusty stopped the folks from coming down here and nailing your hide to the door, then burning your house down on it. Happen there comes a next time he might not be here to stop it, or if he is here allow that you had your warning and stay out of it.'

'So?'

'So this, mister,' drawled Waco. 'From here to there and back the long way you'll not find another man who could stop them folks, happen they get riled up. So don't count on being saved next time.'

And saying that Waco turned on his heel to walk from the room. Gurd sat at his desk for a long time. Then he pushed back his chair and came to his feet. He decided to look around town and see if he could smooth over the trouble left by Gallom.

Gurd was no fighting man, much preferring to use his charm and wits to keep him from trouble. He had not known the plans Gallom had formed and had never really liked the other man. Now Gallom lay dead on a slab in the undertaker's shop. The six deputies had all left town, or were in the process of doing so by the time Gurd reached the jail and somehow the agent felt pleased to see them go.

71

CHAPTER EIGHT

I WANT RAYBOLD DEAD!

Frank Gurd had much work to do before the arrival of the afternoon stage. He must straighten out the mess, calm down the hurt feelings and the anger of the town against the Lazy J. He did not want for his boss to arrive and find a hostile town over which he had no control.

First Gurd went to the undertaker's shop and made arrangements for a first-class burying job to be performed on old Sam Chord. The old-timer lived alone, had no kin and such a gesture would be appreciated by the town.

From the undertaker's shop Gurd headed for Big Ethel's place where he paid for all damage caused by Gallom's deputies and a considerable sum over for the injuries inflicted on the persons of Big Ethel and Whitey. Gurd turned on all his charm and at best he could talk a bird down out of a tree. He talked to good advantage, not only soothing Whitey's annoyed feelings but warming Big Ethel to him. She dug out a bottle of her best whisky and encouraged Gurd to drink, then stated her complete willingness to have all her games checked to make sure she relied on nothing more potent than the house percentage to make a profit on the gambling. Lastly she gave her assurance that the dude visitors would receive the same treatment as her old friends from the town and surrounding ranches. None of them would be over-charged, cold-decked, rolled or in any way molested on her premises.

While Gurd had been long in a line of business which did not tend to make a man believe anything he heard, he did not doubt Big Ethel told the truth. By the time Gurd left the saloon he had done much to wipe out the hatred stirred up by Gus Gallom and which might have made trouble for the Lazy J.

Proof of the success of his appeasement showed when he

made his way to the Wells Fargo office to await the arrival of the stage after lunch. He mingled with the group of people who gathered either to meet friends, collect mail or small freight, or just to be on hand if anybody new and interesting arrived. Gurd found the people friendly and he wondered if his boss would feel satisfied on arrival.

The big Concord stage came rolling into town, its team of horses making good time as they knew the work of the day would soon be over. On the box the driver cracked his whip and the guard slid his double barrel ten guage into the boot, knowing he would have no further need for it that day.

Before the Wells Fargo office, with a cracking flourish of his whip, a haul back on the reins and a boot slamming home the brake, the driver brought his team to a halt. Dust churned under hooves, then settled. The crowd looked expectantly towards the coach door as it opened. They could see a full load of passengers and wondered what new faces would appear.

Johnny Raybold jumped down first. No longer did he wear the leather coat, or carry his gun concealed. Now he dressed for the range and the old 1860 Army Colt rode in the low tied holster. He turned and helped Paulette Defluer down and the young woman looked relieved to be out of the rocking, bouncing coach at last.

Defluer jumped down next. At that moment Gurd came up. He remembered his orders and greeted Drinkwater as a guest, not as employer.

'Mr. Drinkwater?' he asked.

'I'm Drinkwater, this is Mr. Defluer.'

'Pleased to know you, sir,' Gurd said, turning to Defluer on being corrected for his 'mistake'. 'If your party would care to go to my office I'll see about arranging transport to the ranch.'

Unloading Drinkwater's luggage took time for it filled the boot behind the coach.

'I'll see to having it taken to the office,' Gurd said.

'Hey, Johnny, Johnny Raybold!'

Johnny turned and found a familiar face bearing down on him. He grinned and held out his hand to the Wells Fargo agent.

'Why, howdy, Phil. Say how come you-all ended up in

73

Diggers Wells, did the company catch you out?'

'Naw,' scoffed the agent. 'They promoted me in to here. Head office thinks this dude spread'll increase freight and trade in town and they want a good man on hand.'

'Couldn't they find one?'

'You get funnier every old time I see you. Say, this ain't your range. You fixing to head over to the O.D. Connected?'

This was a subject Johnny did not wish to discuss before Drinkwater. He knew the words would carry to Drinkwater's ears and guessed the small man stood listening and watching in that cold cat-cautious way. There was no evading the issue for Phil knew how things stood between Wedge and the O.D. Connected.

'Thought you might. I mind the fun you used to have with Cap'n Fog and his boys at the end of a drive.'

Drinkwater and Defluer exchanged glances. They heard the words and read the implication behind them. Apparently Johnny Raybold was not the sworn enemy of Dusty Fog, he appeared to be a friend. Drinkwater's silence on the true purpose of their visit looked like a wise measure.

'Sure had us some fun,' agreed Johnny. 'Say, where'd a man get a hoss in town here?'

'Try the livery barn down the street. I've got work to do, come on over and have a drink one night,' replied the Wells Fargo official. 'How'd the trip go this time, driver?'

Johnny turned on his heel and looked at the two eastern men. He smiled and said, 'Likely you got the wrong idea about Dusty and the Rio Hondo boys. Sure they play a mite rough and wild at times, but there's no harm in them. They'll not make fuss for you unless you start it first, and that I don't see happening. Thought I'd come down here with you and introduce you, happen you expected the Rio Hondo boys to make fuss for you. I'll be headed over the O.D. Connected, would you want me to bring Dusty over and have him straighten things out with you?'

'If you wish, Johnny,' Drinkwater replied. 'I heard the Rio Hondo men did not take to strangers and that they wanted to buy the Lazy J. Naturally I thought they might make trouble in that case.'

'Sure, only they wouldn't want the Lazy J, it doesn't touch their line and they've land enough as it is. You'll get

74

to know cowhands when you've been out here a spell, find they're good folks.'

'But I thought you said you ran Dusty Fog out of Abilene one time,' Defluer put in, sounding indignant.

'Why sure. Old Dusty took off with my tobacco and I ran him clear back to his camp to get it back again. And as for being scared of him, well, I've no cause to be, we're pards.'

'I'm looking forward to meeting Captain Fog,' Drinkwater remarked. 'Bring him over any time.'

'I'll do that,' promised Johnny, turning on his heel. 'See you down trail.'

Drinkwater watched the tall young Texan walk away. Then he turned to where Gurd had helped to tote the baggage. He made a sign and they headed across the street to the Lazy J's building.

'Where's your private quarters?' Drinkwater asked.

'In back here, Boss,' Gurd replied. 'I'll have the wagon ready to take you out to the ranch. The men are waiting.'

One thing a girl of Paulette's class learned real early was to know when her presence might prove embarrassing. She asked for the ladies' room and headed for it so as to leave her father and Drinkwater free to discuss whatever bothered them.

'That cowhand knows too much, Gurd,' Drinkwater said as they entered the small back room.

'You mean about the ranch?'

'That and my personal business. He has to be stopped reaching the O.D. Connected. Can you have it done?'

Defluer licked his lips nervously. He had never seen this side of Drinkwater before. The small man stood calmy suggesting the death of another human being, for that was what the words amounted to.

'He knows nothing of our plans,' Defluer protested weakly.

'Only that for some reason we feared the O.D. Connected and wished to have along a man who was not afraid of Dusty Fog. When the trouble comes it would be a starting point, a place for the other side to look if they became suspicious. The story I told Raybold might lull his suspicions now, but not later. How about it, Gurd, can we prevent Raybold leaving town?'

'No, Boss.'

'Why not, I thought you had the local law in your hands.'

'I had. Only Gallom wanted to make some money on the side by taking over the saloon in town. He started to abuse the owner, a well-liked woman, in the street and Dusty Fog stopped him.'

'Well?' growled Drinkwater.

'There was some shooting.'

'And?' asked Drinkwater, thinking of the splendid references Gallom brought, including comments on his skill with a gun.

'Gallom's dead.'

'Dead?' croaked Defluer. 'You mean Dusty Fog murdered him?'

'Killed him,' corrected Gurd, not knowing who Defluer might be, but guessing he had some part in Drinkwater's plans or he would not be present and hearing a highly confidential conversation. 'There's a lot of difference in murdering and killing. Gallom murdered an old man just before Dusty Fog returned and shot him down. Folks were riled up about the way Gallom acted. I managed to quieten them down.'

'And you don't control the town any more?' Drinkwater said. 'I thought Gallom had six men backing him.'

'He had. They left town right after the shooting, didn't even stop to collect their pay.'

'Then there's no law in town?'

'No, Boss.'

'It should be easy enough to handle Raybold then.'

Gurd shook his head. 'I told you, boss, folks are riled about Gallom and blaming the Lazy J for him being here. I quietened things down. But the folks won't stand for another killing, especially if they think we're involved in it.'

A knock came at the outside of the door. Gurd opened it and the two men from the Lazy J entered. They looked a couple of hard-cases, and they wore their guns tied low and didn't appear to be the sort who would be overly bothered by scruples.

'You ready to head for the spread?' one asked Gurd.

'This is your boss,' Gurd replied.

Both men threw Drinkwater a calculating glance. He studied them, then made a decision.

'Bill Acre hired you,' he said, making a statement of it.

'Told us to come down this way.'

'How'd you like to make a bonus for yourself?'

'Doing what?' asked the taller man.

'Making sure that cowhand who came in on the stage doesn't reach the O.D. Connected house. It's worth two hundred dollars each.'

The men exchanged glances. 'In town?' asked one.

'Well clear of town. Make it look like a hold-up. You'd better use your bandanas as masks when you hit him, just in case anybody should see you.'

'You just hired two men,' drawled the smaller man.

'Sure, pay up and we'll tend to his needings.'

'Do you know the man?' Defluer asked, wondering if all their problems might be so easily solved.

'Nope.'

'He's tall, red-haired, wearing a dark green shirt. He'll be on a livery barn horse,' Drinkwater said. 'Don't forget. I want Raybold dead—but I don't want to be tied into it in any way.'

Although Johnny Raybold had no idea of Drinkwater's true feelings he wasted none of his time in Diggers Wells.

Whistling a cowhand tune he rode from town. He kept to the well marked trail and did not notice that a couple of riders followed him, riding the rims on either side of the trail, keeping parallel to it and making sure they showed as little of themselves as possible.

Johnny had no idea that Drinkwater might be plotting either his death or trouble with the O.D. Connected. He accepted the small man's story and thought little about the matter. Instead he thought of real range cooking, of food brought out the way he loved—in large quantities, for Johnny had long been noted for his ability at a dining table. Likely there would be a meal going when he hit the O.D. Connected, even if there was not the cook would raise something for him.

Ahead of him the Rio Hondo water glinted in the sun. He pressed the horse on towards the river bank. Here the trail had been churned up by unnumbered hooves for this was the main crossing point between Polveroso and Rio Hondo County and the town of Diggers Wells.

'Let's get us over, old hoss,' Johnny said.

In the distance, at least a mile away, hounds bayed their trail song. Johnny slowed the brown and listened to the music of the chase, the crashing bawl of hounds as they ran a line. Over the river somebody was hunting, trailing a pack of blue-ticks from the sound of it. Next to food Johnny loved hunting with a pack of good hounds more than any other thing.

'Be those Rio Hondo varmints,' he drawled to the brown horse. 'Listen to those hounds sing through. Wonder if I can find whoever's running them?'

The horse splashed into the shallow water, having made the crossing enough times to know it held no dangers. Johnny sat easily, yet he kept alert for he did not know the horse and wondered how it handled in water.

On the rim, at the right side, one of the Lazy J men drew his rifle and lifted it to his shoulder. He lined down on Johnny as the horse splashed through the ford. Hit right the young Texan's body might be washed downstream and never be found at all. The shot, coming from a range of over a hundred yards, would strike home without warning, with luck the cowhand would never know what hit him.

The rider on the far slope saw his pard draw the rifle and could have cursed. He hoped to get in much closer before he cut loose but he did not dare shout out for fear of alerting Johnny.

With his bandana drawn up over the lower half of his face the first man felt hot and uncomfortable. He lined his rifle on Johnny's back but the sweat ran into his sighting eye and blurred it. Angrily he wiped his face, then aimed again. His finger closed on the trigger. Under him the horse moved uneasily, just a little—but enough.

Lead screamed by Johnny's ear. He heard the slap of the close passing bullet, saw dirt erupt from the Rio Hondo County bank and heard the flat crack of a rifle from behind him.

He reacted almost without thinking. Spurs rammed into the flanks of the brown causing it to leap forward. Another shot came by, from the other side of the trail to the first. The bullet churned up water to one side of Johnny, then the brown went running, churning through the shallow water. Leaning forward Johnny jerked out the Winchester rifle from his saddle boot.

The brown horse slipped, going down. Only just in time Johnny kicked his legs clear and left the saddle. He lit down thigh deep in water, but he lit down on the run. From behind he heard yells and hooves, knew his attackers, whoever they might be, were riding closer, to a range where a Winchester could do most good, or harm, depending on which end of the weapon a man stood.

Nothing slowed a running man so effectively as water. Johnny churned ahead, expecting at any moment to feel lead slam into him. Behind him the brown made its feet and followed him, reins dangling but floating on the water and not stopping the horse. Likely the horse standing saved Johnny's life for it got between him and the rifles of the two men.

Now Johnny made the shallows, then felt sand under his feet. Two shots came by him and he lit down rolling. Ahead of him, by the side of the trail, stood a small rock. It wasn't what a man would pick to hide behind, happen he'd got good cover to choose from.

But to Johnny, being the only cover on hand, that little hunk of rock sure looked like safety.

Landing behind the rock Johnny twisted around, his rifle peeping around the side as he studied the situation.

'Owlhoots!' he growled, seeing two masked men hurriedly leave their saddles and take cover at the far side of the river. 'They'll sure earn anything they get from lil ole me.'

Behind Johnny the land sloped up wooded and safe if he could get to it. Only there happened to be a good twenty yards of open land before he hit the safety of those same wooded slopes and a man would offer a real good target as he tried to cross it.

'Dang fool hoss,' growled Johnny, watching the brown come ashore well downstream of him, then amble forward a few steps and halt. 'Why in hell don't you either come closer, or go right off so you don't tempt me. I bet ole Dusty had the training of you.'

He waited for more shots but neither men looked like they aimed to use ammunition on him. Nor did they look like they aimed to pull out and let him ride free. Well, happen they wanted to play Injuns they'd picked the right boy to do it with. For all his red hair Johnny Raybold could act cool

79

and didn't run short of patience easily. He could wait until they made their play, or night gave him a chance of getting clear.

The two men across the river could see how Johnny's hand lay. They knew how little chance they would have of getting Johnny from his place. Then one of them pointed upstream. He darted from his pard's side, hitting the far side of the trail. Up there, given a mite of luck, a man could lay a right true bead down on the Texan, have him under a gun and exposed as a lizard on a flat-topped rock.

CHAPTER NINE

BETTY HARDIN INTERVENES

When Dusty Fog, Mark Counter, the Ysabel Kid and Waco did not return with the rest of the ranch crew Betty expressed herself in language unbecoming of a lady of gentle upbringing. She hoped her cousin would help with the hunt, although only for company. She and Dusty were closer than brother and sister, had always been that way. Betty liked nothing more than to ride with Dusty when the hounds called in the woods. She did not need help in the hunting, or company because she feared the cougar she hunted. Betty knew she could rely on the four big blue-tick hounds and the wicked little .44.40 Winchester Model 1873 carbine she carried.

After Red and Sue departed for the town of Polveroso and more social calls, Betty gathered her bay horse, a horse which had stood up to cougar hunts before, and the hounds. She rode out, making for the cougar's last kill. In this she missed Dusty's return and he found himself caught by his uncle to check some accounts.

Apparently the cougar had been back to its kill and fed during the night. The hounds were scattered but Strike, the big leader, father of the other two dog hounds, knew what a dead colt meant. He advanced towards the remains, dropping his nose and smelled at the grass. He swung around the horse's remains, then went rigid on his legs, back hair standing stiff and bristly. He threw back his head and gave out with a bellow which brought the other hounds to him. Belle, the bitch, Blinker and Joe, her two pups, now full grown, joined Strike, their noses checking the scent before they too gave tongue and let their mistress know they had hit on the cougar's line.

'Yahoo!' Betty yelled. 'Lay to it, dogs!'

They needed no second bidding. The scent held well, not red hot, but enough to allow a good pace for the following hounds. Those four blue-ticks would run only cougar or bear. On a line they would ignore deer or any other creature but the two species of predator they were trained to hunt.

From the kill Betty's hounds headed across fairly open range, but they made for where the woods closed in. On the open land she could keep up behind them, especially while they ran the old trail. Once in the trees, and when they pushed the cougar out of hiding, the horse had never been sired which could keep up with her blue-tick pack.

Betty did not even try. She guessed the cougar must be a young and inexperienced tom. The four blue-ticks could handle such a cougar, might even finish the job without her aid. They fought as a team and Belle, smallest and lightest, weighed sixty-five pounds. The dogs stretched up from there to Strike's eighty pounds of power and fight savvy. They knew how to fight, when to back off and let the cornered animal run through their ranks, to give chase once more.

So the girl concentrated on keeping on the same line the hounds followed, listening to their trail music ringing out through the woods. She knew the range like the back of her hand, could tell the cougar headed towards the Rio Hondo, swinging down to the south well below the Diggers Wells ford. She rode at an easy lope, saving her horse in case a dash should become necessary.

'Dangnab and blast it to hell and gone,' said Betty, mildly for her under the circumstances. 'That fool cat'll run clear out of the county the way it's going.'

Already the sound of the hounds died off into the distance. Betty drew her horse to a halt and listened to the fading sounds. She knew as much about cougar hunting as many a predator hunter who made his living tracking stock killers. The young cougar would try to stay ahead of the pack, then when they closed might take to a tree. If that happened Betty must get to the pack, let them know she backed them up. She decided to swing out towards the river, follow the high country and listen for the hounds to bay treed.

The flat bark of rifles came to Betty's ears. She halted the horse and looked around her. The hound music, still running, sounded far to the south and the cougar could not be back in this direction as yet. There were more shots, coming from down by the ford or she did not know this country.

A more prudent young woman might have ignored the sound, or headed the other way, but Betty never acted in a manner likely to be called prudent. She wondered who might be shooting down that close to the trail and with Betty to wonder was to take a look.

She came into sight of the ford and looked down, seeing a cowhand flattened in the inadequate cover of a rock, right out in the open at the river's edge. He held a rifle, but did not seem to be shooting at the man across the river.

Betty studied everything. Then she saw the man on the far shore's face was masked. A man didn't hide his features under a drawn-up bandana without good cause, and one of the best causes was because he aimed to commit robbery. The girl decided to throw in her assistance to the cowhand. Then a movement caught the corner of her eye. It took Betty a long second to pick up what attracted her attention in the first place. Then she saw it.

A second man, also masked or she missed her guess, crawled towards a bush on the far side of the river. It took Betty less than a second to see why he made for this particular bit of cover. In the time for realisation to hit, Betty left her saddle and lit down on her right knee, resting her left elbow on the raised left knee. There would be no time to take fancy aim for that second man could see the cowhand, had him under a gun.

Squinting along the barrel of her carbine Betty lined the sights and touched off a shot. At that range, with the short barrelled Winchester carbine she would need luck to make a fast-taken hit. Not that she wanted to hit, only to scare the man and warn him off.

In this she succeeded admirably. The bullet slapped over the gunman's head even as he lined on Johnny Raybold and warned him that another player had entered the game, one in a position to copper any bets he made.

Johnny Raybold also heard the shot from behind him but kept still. The bullet did not come near him and he was more likely to find a friend than an enemy on this side of the Rio Hondo. Then he heard a yell from upstream and realised how close he had been to departing from this world on the end of a bullet.

'Get out of it!' yelled one man from across the river.

They pulled back, sliding through cover until reaching their horses. Then both hit the saddles fast and headed back in the way they came. Johnny stayed where he lay behind the rock. This might even yet be a trick, the rifle on the rim could be waiting for a chance to pump lead into him, the owlhoots running to lure him out into the open.

Hooves sounded on the slope, coming towards him through the bushes as the men beyond the river disappeared. Johnny turned and saw the approaching rider, but not clearly enough. He thought it might be a boy, the shadows hid any clear sight.

'Thanks, boy,' he said.

'Mister,' replied the most unboy-like voice. 'Either you need glasses, or I'm not the girl I thought I was.'

Then she came into sight and Johnny bit down an exclamation of surprise, apology and admiration. He had never seen Betty Hardin but he could recollect the way the O.D. Connected boys described her. Johnny grinned the grin which made him famous along the cattle trails.

'You're a gal and I sure don't need glasses, ma'am,' he said. 'Allow you're Betty Hardin, aren't you?'

'Likely. Let's pull back away from this open land, your friends might be back. Or were they a couple of irate fathers?'

'Landsakes, no, I steer clear of them,' Johnny answered and headed for the brown horse, catching its reins. He swung into the saddle and waved a hand to his mount. 'They sure didn't have much choice in the Diggers Wells livery barn.'

No cowhand worth his salt would want to have a pretty gal think he couldn't run to better than that brown plug, especially a girl who knew top hands and was allowed by her friends to be as good as their best with cattle.

'I thought maybe those pair were trying to wideloop such a valuable critter, friend,' Betty answered. 'It's none of my business and I hate nosey females, so I'm not going to ask why that pair were after you. Why were they?'

'You're worse'n the Kid for talking two ways at once,' Johnny grinned. 'They maybe allowed that I'd make good pickings. Say, you are Betty Hardin, aren't you?'

'Why sure, how did you know?'

'I heard tell about you from various folks. Like how you can outcuss Ole Devil and Dusty both. How you're as bad for running hound-dawgs than any of that dawg-running bunch. How you got a temper that's real likely to burst red hot and ornery—and how you make the best biscuits in Texas.'

Betty eyed the straight-faced Johnny as he ran through a catalogue of her virtues and wound up with the main topic in his book.

'Who told you all that?' she asked.

'I'm no snitch. You won't get me to tell you it was the Kid, Mark, Waco. So it's no use you trying to bribe me with none of them biscuits, happen you got a few on you.'

She studied him again, dropping her eyes to his Army Colt after examining his red hair. Her finger stabbed out at his chest.

'Johnny Raybold,' she said. 'You must be him. Hair as red as Cousin Red's, too mean to buy a Peacemaker and all stomach clean down to your boots. And I'm not going to tell you it was the Kid who told me about you.' She changed the pointing finger to a hand held out to be shaken. 'Right pleased to meet you.'

The hand which clamped on to Betty's felt hard, firm and she liked the general look of the cowhand from the Wedge.

'About them biscuits?' he asked hopefully.

'Why sure, I've some in the saddle-bags. Just don't die of starvation until we hit the top of the slope.'

'I'll try, ma'am——!'

'*Mr.* Raybold, are you sure Cousin Dusty is your friend?' Betty interrupted in a cold voice.

'Why sure!' replied Johnny in a startled tone.

'Thought you were close strangers. Any man who's a friend of Cousin Dusty can call me Betty.'

'I'd like that fine, ma—Betty.'

She threw a glance at him and just a hint of a blush came to her cheeks. It died off but left Betty feeling slightly flustered. Why would she be sat there blushing like a naïve backwoods schoolgirl just because a cowhand showed pleasure at being allowed to use her name?

'How about those two owlhoots?' she asked, more to hide her confusion than because she had interest in them.

'Let 'em go. Time we could throw up a posse and take after them they'll be long and far gone.'

'Why'd they pick on you?' she inquired.

'Don't ask me. I'd only just rolled into Diggers on the afternoon stage and I sure hadn't thrown my wad about in plain view. Say, about them biscuits?'

'Landsakes!' gasped Betty, opening her saddle-bag and digging out a small linen bag. 'Here, dip in and take one.'

He did as bid, removing a biscuit and raising it to his mouth. Then Johnny sat fast, the biscuit hovering between his lips. He stared ahead, and so did Betty, the same thought in both minds.

'They've turned him and he's running back this way!' Betty said, stuffing the bag away again and listening to the approaching sound of hound music.

'Lordy lord!' Johnny replied, lowering the biscuit, a look of rapture in his eyes. 'Just listen to those dogs sing out.'

'It's real beautiful, isn't it,' she replied. 'There's nothing like the song of a blue-tick to my ears.'

'Or mine. Some folks allow a redbone or a Plott can sing better, but they don't know sic 'em about hound-dawgs.'

Suddenly the note of the music changed. No longer did the loud, steady trail chop echo and ring through the woods, the note deepened, turned more coarse and excited in pitch. Neither Betty nor Johnny needed a book to tell them what this meant.

'They've treed him!' Betty yelled, lifting the carbine free. 'They got that fool ole cat up there on a limb, Johnny boy.'

'Then what're we waiting for, gal?' Johnny replied. 'Put those petmakers to work and get at it.'

His advice came a mite too late. A full second before his last word came out Betty was putting her petmaker spurs to appropriate use. The bay horse, fretting in impatience, wasted no more time but lit out for the sound of hound music on the jump.

'Man, oh man!' thought Johnny, watching Betty head for the trees at a racing gallop. 'Johnny boy, you found a real gal.'

Not knowing of Johnny's thoughts Betty concentrated on keeping her seat and letting the bay make good time. It didn't do the hound pack's confidence any good to leave them bawling treed for longer than was necessary. They relied on Betty to get up and take care of things for them once they'd run that old cougar up a tree. She knew the hounds would stay there bawling treed until the cougar jumped and ran again, but she never liked delaying getting to them. The bay horse knew that, could read the trail calls as good as its rider. It also knew to take the shortest possible time to get to the location of the sound.

The way Betty stuck on her horse, keeping it running, bending low to avoid branches which might have swept her from the saddle, adjusting her weight to fast turns or fancy side-steps which avoided tree trunks, showed Johnny the O.D. Connected hadn't called it wrong when they claimed Betty could stay afork anything with hair and out-ride most men.

Betty saw Strike through the trees ahead and brought her bay to a halt as she got her first view of the quarry. The cougar had treed in a stout old chestnut tree, standing on a lower limb, tawny, lithe and beautiful in its savage splendour, tail lashing from side to side and jaws drawn in a spitting snarl at the dogs below. The pack still kept their tree chop ringing out. Blinker and Joe reared back on hind legs, forepaws against the tree trunk, heads thrown back and jaws working in a chop cry. Belle and Strike, older, more wise in the ways of cougar, circled and waited, throwing their voice to bring their mistress to them.

On seeing the approach of a human being the cougar jumped. It sailed out and away from the tree, going a good thirty feet or more, to land on cat-paws and start to run once more.

Against younger, less experienced hounds the trick might have worked, gained vital ground for the cougar. Betty's four blue-ticks knew cougar tricks, they knew what sort of animal they followed, one still young and untried in the art of dog-evasion. So, even as the cougar leapt, Strike swung forward. Almost as soon as the cougar landed Strike was after him, crowding in on the left flank, eighty pounds of snarling, savage fury. Belle came racing in from the right, jaws slashing and fighting snarl ringing free.

The cat swung around, facing them, unsheathing its claws and lashing out. Belle seemed to almost take a back somersault to start clear. The other three piled in, swinging to the flanks and rear, not facing the ripping claws. Belle

87

stayed up front, keeping clear and screaming out canine abuse at the cougar, holding its attention from the others.

With a low snarl the cougar took the line of least resistance, charging at Belle. The bitch let him come, then at the last moment threw herself aside, letting him pass. Now the cougar headed straight for Betty and behind it the hounds closed in once more.

Betty started to lift the carbine, but not even a well trained horse like the bay would stand up in the face of that snarling, spitting, charging devil-cat. Giving a snort the bay danced restlessly and Betty clung on one handed, not aiming to drop the carbine at such a moment.

'Yeeah!' she yelled. 'Turn him, boys!'

Like a streak of lightning Joe boiled in, charging from the cougar's side and slamming into his flank. Dog and cougar went down, rolling over, but Joe knew a heap better than keep hanging on. He went rolling clear, missing a raking claw by scant inches. The cougar came up fast, snarling, spitting its hate and slashing at the rest of the pack as they crashed in to keep it away from Joe and give the dog time to rise.

Making another of those long, sailing bounds, the cougar took off over the heads of the dogs. Strike leapt up, jaws clashing and body twisting in his effort to take the cougar in mid-flight, missed and he dropped to the ground once more. On landing, the cougar ran a few yards, then went up the side of another tree. Blinker and Belle were in close, they leapt, both aiming for the down-hanging tail, missed and came together to crash down snarling and snapping. Then Blinker realised who he attacked and leapt clear of his mother's powerful snapping jaws.

'Dang fool dogs!' yelled Betty. 'Watch that cat!'

At that moment Johnny arrived, cursing his brown horse and threatening all kinds of revenge when next he saw its owner. He saw the cougar take to a tree once more and yelled his encouragement to the hounds.

'It's your cat, girl,' he said to Betty.

Raising the carbine, Betty sighted and fired. She knew her work. The cougar slid down from its limb, pitching to the ground and landing limp at the foot of the tree. Betty's bullet went through the head, right where she intended it. There was no pain, no thrashing in agony of a wound. Just the one shot and the cougar's stock killing days ended.

Instantly, the moment the cougar landed, all four hounds sprang at it. So did Betty, yelling angry and profane commands which somehow did not seem profane the way she threw them in spluttering fury at the blue-ticks.

'Get the living hell out of it, you fool critters!' she yelled. 'Landsakes, don't sit there on your butt-end like you're waiting for the spring rains!' Betty howled at Johnny. 'Get afoot and help me knock some sense into these fool hounds!'

Leaving the saddle in a bound Johnny ran forward and grabbed the nearest hound, hauling him back. The dog, Blinker, swung his head and chopped at Johnny's arm, then yelped as Betty thudded him hard in the ribs with the gun butt. Blinker took a jump to one side, having received warning that his mistress's temper touched danger point. The other hounds saw this also and fell back, sinking to the ground and watching Betty.

So was Johnny. Watching her and feeling as he had never before felt about any girl. He knew the feeling could never amount to anything. Betty Hardin, grand-daughter of the owner of the biggest ranch in Texas was not for him. He had enough money saved to buy in on a small spread, but the spread he bought would be no bigger than the O.D. Connected's lower forty. Even if she liked him he could hardly expect a girl like Betty Hardin to be interested in him.

'He's a beauty,' Johnny said.

Betty nodded. Johnny and she looked at each other, their eyes met and suddenly both were laughing.

'You sure told those hounds, Betty,' he said.

'Like the teacher at that fancy eastern school used to tell us,' Betty replied. 'A young lady should be known for her clarity of diction and the way she can turn a phrase.'

'I wouldn't know what that meant,' drawled Johnny. 'But I reckon she might have been right. I'll skin out that old cat for you.'

The girl gave him no argument. In the past, on lone hunts, she had skinned out her own cats, but never really liked the chore. Her eyes watched him as he went to his horse, dug out the bedroll and produced a Comanche scalping knife.

CHAPTER TEN

WE'RE HAVING NO FUSS WITH THEM

'You met up with Cousin Dusty in Quiet Town, didn't you?' Betty asked as they let the horses water at a small stream close to where the cougar fell before her carbine.

'Sure. Doc Leroy and Rusty Willis were his deputies and we tied on in to help them out at the end.'

They came riding down towards the O.D. Connected's main buildings before either of them really noticed where they were. It came as something of a surprise to look up and see the corrals ahead. And a disappointment to Johnny. He would soon be in the bunkhouse among his friends, but he would also be no more than another cowhand passing through and receiving traditional hospitality.

'I'll expect you up the house for dinner,' Betty said. 'You needn't worry about dressing, we don't.'

A blush came to Johnny's face. 'Gee thanks, Betty.'

'I'm only doing it to have somebody on hand to tell how I got the cougar,' she replied. 'The Kid never believes I ran one down but I've got proof this time.'

At that moment Mark Counter came walking from the main house with Waco at his side. He looked down to the corral and spoke in a tone which carried to the new arrivals.

'Hey, Waco, you'd best go and warn Jimmo to lock up all the food, Johnny Raybold's here.'

'I'll do just that,' agreed Waco.

Betty glared at the two men as they advanced to the corral. 'You pair of sheep,' she bellowed. 'That's no way to treat a guest.'

'He's not a guest,' Mark objected. 'He's a pest.'

The handshakes which greeted Johnny showed that his greeting so far had been far from sincere.

'If you pair were anything like gentlemen, you'd take care of the horses for us,' Betty remarked, then she looked at the buggy standing before the house. 'See we've got callers. Uncle Hondo come out with Aunt Betsy?'

'Sure,' Mark agreed.

'We'd best tell him about you, Johnny,' she remarked.

'Shucks, ole Johnny don't want jailing, he'd lower the tone of the place,' put in Waco.

'How'd you like bouncing all around the corral on your lil pumpkin head?' Betty asked coldly. 'It'd lower your tone some.'

'Come on, boy,' drawled Mark. 'She's getting all uppy again. Take hold of the brown. Man, this's a better hoss than you usually fork, Johnny.'

At that moment a considerable racket arose from the bunkhouse, drawing Betty's and her three companions' attention to it. First a cowhand sailed through the open door, lighting down bouncing on his rump, then a struggling cluster of figures followed him. Half-a-dozen of the spread's younger workers milled around Dusty Fog in an attempt to teach him the error of his ways. Suddenly strange things began to happen. Dusty's hands or feet stabbed out, taking hold, hooking and pushing at his assailants, at which one after another would flip through the air or tumble to the ground.

'Damned if that mean ole Dusty ain't abusing them poor fellers again,' Waco remarked, throwing a suggestive look at Johnny as he remembered hearing something about the visitor.

'He ought to be stopped,' Johnny declared. 'And I'm the one to stop him.'

Ever since the first time he had seen Dusty's *ju jitsu* and *karate* performed, Johnny had had an ambition. Helped by his Wedge pard, Rusty Willis, he had repeatedly set out to prove that the fancy 'Chinese' tricks could not lick good old U.S. wrestling.* That the pair's attempts invariably ended in failure had done little to dampen the red-head's ambition.

Seeing Dusty occupied in dealing with the cowhands, and presenting his back, struck Johnny as a gift sent by providence and not to be missed. Darting forward, Johnny swiftly passed his hands under Dusty's arm-pits, to interlink his fingers behind the small blond's neck for a full nelson hold.

* One occasion is told in *Trigger Fast*.

91

'Now I've got y——!' Johnny began in delight.

Dusty acted with his usual speed, bowing his torso away from his captor and raising his arms over his head. Then he snapped the arms down with some force and rammed his buttocks hard into the red-head's belly. Letting out a gasp, Johnny opened his fingers and felt his arms forced apart as he bent involuntarily forward above Dusty. From freeing himself of Johnny's full nelson, Dusty's arms reached back to catch the other's head. With a wail of distress, Johnny passed over Dusty's right shoulder and landed on the recumbent bodies of two cowhands.

'That's maybe how they "get" folks where Johnny comes from,' Waco commented.

Annoyance flickered on Betty's face as she left Mark's and Waco's side. Hearing soft foot-falls behind him, Dusty whirled ready to defend himself. Discovering who approached, he relaxed. On other occasions Betty had taken a hand, using her considerable knowledge of the Oriental fighting arts to help him quell obstreperous cowhands. So it came as a shock to him when she took hold of his left bicep and right wrist, pivoting smoothly into an *ashi-guruma* leg wheel throw. Gliding over the girl's raised right leg, Dusty landed on the ground with a satisfactory—from the assailants', or victims' ears at any rate—thud.

Nor had Betty finished. Her unexpected assault left Dusty too winded and amazed to resist the follow-up. Grabbing his right ankle, she deftly twisted him on to his stomach and finished the move standing astride him, facing his feet and with the trapped leg bent back under her right arm in a painful manner.

'I'll teach you to bully folk!' Betty yelled. 'Say "uncle".'

While the girl did not exert the hold's full pressure, Dusty knew that he could not escape from it without using some extremely dangerous counter. Which left only one course open to him.

'Uncle!' he said.

Thrusting away Dusty's leg, Betty stepped clear. The small Texan rolled over and sat up, looking with surprise at his cousin. Then he saw Johnny Raybold and a grin came to his lips.

'Hey, Johnny,' he greeted. 'I thought you was around.'

'Get up and quit loafing,' Betty ordered. 'Both of you, I

mean. Isn't that Uncle Hondo's horse by the corral?'

'He rode in soon after you left,' Dusty replied.

'And couldn't've picked a better time,' Betty said. In addition to being her uncle and Dusty's father, Hondo Fog was sheriff of Rio Hondo County. 'Let's go and see him.'

Something in the girl's voice warned Dusty that her business with his father might be serious. So he walked towards the house with her and Johnny. Mark and Waco watched them go, while the other cowhands rose and headed for the bunkhouse discussing the surprising turn of events. Much the same thoughts were on Waco's mind as he and Mark led the horses to the corral.

'I never thought to see Betty turn on Dusty like that,' the youngster said.

'One of these days, boy,' Mark answered, 'I'm just going to have to tell you about the birds, the bees and the flowers.'

A superior smile came to Waco's face and he patted Mark on the shoulder in a paternal manner. 'I tell you, son, there's nothing to that story. Why I kept a bird, a bee and a flower in a box for weeks and nothing happened.'

The sound of voices led them to the big gun decorated library. Ole Devil Hardin sat his wheelchair in his favourite place. Facing him, big and powerful looking, Hondo Fog sucked at his pipe and watched the Ysabel Kid who leaned by the open fireplace.

'Never knowed Tortilla hit this far north of the line,' the Kid was saying. 'Which same don't mean he wouldn't.'

'Hernandez isn't often wrong,' Hondo replied. 'He——'

All eyes went to the door of the room. Betty entered first followed by Johnny who received encouragement in the form of a poke in the ribs from Dusty. The girl smiled.

'Go on, and if it's a story I shouldn't hear I'll cover my ears. Anyway I know all the Kid's stories.'

'I'm sorry to disappoint you,' Hondo replied. 'Hernandez brought me word that he saw Tortilla, you know that greaser *bandido*, Dusty saw him down at Phillipe's out by Diggers Wells.'

'Tortilla, huh?' replied Dusty. 'Let's hear Lon on it.'

'We *were* hearing him when you lot burst in,' growled Ole Devil. 'Howdy young Raybold, take a seat.'

'Like Hondo said,' drawled the Kid when the seat-taking

ended, 'Hernandez doesn't often call the play wrong. Sure this's further north than Tortilla usually raids, but word has it the Rangers and the Mexican Guardia Rurale have been running the border bunches ragged for quite a spell now. Likely Tortilla moved out to look for new pastures.'

'I wonder if they were Tortilla's men who tried to jump Johnny by the Diggers' ford,' Betty put in.

Her words brought all eyes to Johnny as he sat at her side. Hondo Fog gave a grunt, then asked:

'What's it all about, Johnny?'

'Like Betty said, couple of masked jaspers jumped me, let off a few shots my way as I crossed the river. I lit down on the other side, laid up behind a rock to wait and see what they was at.'

'Get any?' asked the Kid.

'Nope.'

'You never could shoot worth a cuss.'

'You hush your fat face, Lon Ysabel!' Betty snapped. 'Johnny was laid up there when I came on him. I cut loose from the rim over the ford and they took off again.'

'A lady doesn't tell a gentleman to hush his fat face,' drawled the Kid.

'So who's the gentleman?' Betty replied.

'Would they be Tortilla's men?' Hondo put in, cutting off the remark which rose to the Kid's lips.

'Does he run any northern range stock in his herd?' Johnny replied.

Hondo turned to the Kid as an acknowledged authority on Mexican border bandit gangs.

'Not *gringos*,' replied the Kid. 'Mexican bad hats, all his crew, real *hombre malo* boys.'

'This pair were Americans,' Johnny stated. 'I'd swear on it.'

'Why'd they take after you, Johnny?' asked Hondo.

'I don't know. Weren't after me for money. I'd not showed any I had and I only arrived in Diggers on the stage, left town near on right after.'

'Could be somebody looking for evens,' drawled the Kid.

'Could be, only I can't think of anybody I gave that much cause to hate me.'

'You said they jumped you at the ford,' Dusty drawled. 'You landed our side, they hunkered down on the other and started a long range shooting fuss with you?'

'That's the way it happened.'

Dusty and Hondo exchanged glances. Both possessed a better than fair knowledge of how crooks worked. The happenings at the ford did not fit into their ideas of how a pair of hold-up artists would operate.

'You sure nobody's after you?' Dusty asked.

'I've been north for a spell,' Johnny answered. 'After Stone paid off our last drive I decided to see what New York looked like. I had a mite of trouble up there but that feller wouldn't know my name, or how to find me.'

'Which feller?' Hondo inquired.

'Miller, owns a saloon in New York. I got tangled in some fuss, but he couldn't have followed me, or fixed to have me gunned. Drinkwater said Miller didn't know my name or anything about me.'

'Who?' asked Dusty.

'Little dude, runs that Lazy J spread over to Diggers Wells. At least he's one of the big wheels behind it. I met up with him after the fuss at Miller's, came back with him. Funny thing about him though, Dusty, he seemed tolerable worried about the O.D. Connected causing fuss for the Lazy J. He asked if I knew you. I allowed I did, reckon I made it sound like we weren't *amigos*, told him I wasn't scared of you and he asked me to travel down here with him. So I did. Hoped to find out a mite more about why he was worried, but he never mentioned it again.'

'Then he never said why he thought we might cause fuss for him?' asked Dusty.

Johnny shook his head. 'Never a word. When we hit town I aimed to hang on for a spell, learn what I could. Only I got recognised in town and Drinkwater learned I wasn't so much an enemy of yours after all.'

'How'd he act when he heard?' Hondo put in.

'Same as always, calm, friendly without ever making friends, if you know what I mean. Like he accepted a man, but didn't ever want him to become real friendly. He said he's heard the O.D. Connected wanted to buy the Lazy J and thought you might make a fuss for him. I explained things out, then left town.'

'We're having no fuss with them,' Ole Devil remarked. 'The Lazy J'd be no good to us even if we needed more land.'

'That's what I told him, sir,' replied Johnny. 'Told him I'd bring Dusty on over to straighten things out and he agreed.'

'He set a date for me to go over?' asked Dusty.

'Nope, just left it at that. You don't think he was the one who came after me, do you?'

Dusty shrugged. 'Not knowing the gent I couldn't say. Only you said there were two of them and Drinkwater's only one man, unless he's something unusual, two for the price of one.'

'He's not,' grinned Johnny.

'And those pair weren't dudes either,' Betty went on. 'They were western stock even if we wouldn't take either of them on as cook's louse.'

At that moment Tommy Okasi entered the room, carrying a tray with bottles of beer and glasses. Betty told the small man there would be another for dinner and he left the room to warn Jimmo and fetch along another glass for Johnny.

Talk welled up again, the Kid promised to keep his eyes open for any sign of Tortilla and Hondo gave his opinion that it would be worse than useless to try hunting the two men now. It would be dark soon and long before pursuit could be arranged, the two men would be well hidden.

Then serious talk ended. Betty found she did not need to introduce Johnny to her grandfather and got involved in an argument with the Kid about her hunting prowess. Time passed quickly, the more quickly for one Johnny Raybold, late scout for the Wedge trail crew and who now sought for excuses to stay on in Rio Hondo County so as to be nearer the black haired and beautiful little girl who came so suddenly, violently and with such impact into his life.

'Anyways,' the Kid's voice suddenly came to Johnny's ears. 'There's a black bear running the river country who'd whup the pants off your fool hounds.'

'Yeah?' demanded Betty belligerently. 'We can take him any ole time. Can't we, Johnny?'

Johnny agreed with alacrity. He forgot all his other plans. It looked like Betty wanted him to stay on in the Rio Hondo country for a spell. From the grins on the faces of her kin and their friends the invitation was not entirely unwelcome with them either.

CHAPTER ELEVEN

A SLOW KILLER AT WORK

At about the same time as Betty Hardin and Johnny Raybold foregathered in the O.D. Connected's house kitchen to wash the dinner dishes, Basil Drinkwater received a visit from the two men he sent after the young Texan.

The room at the Lazy J had been furnished to meet his fastidious tastes in such matters long before his arrival and reserved strictly for his personal use. His manager, a man with considerable knowledge in the running of a top-class hotel, came to bring the men before their boss, making sure none of the other guests saw this for Drinkwater did not wish his connections with the ownership known.

'How did it go?' he asked. 'Is Raybold dead?'

He spoke with a bluntness the two men found hard to stomach. Both were paid gunmen who made their living fighting for other people. Yet the people for whom they previously worked showed a marked reluctance to come straight to the point in such a case. True they were alone in the room, the manager having been dismissed, but it still shook them. In all matters Drinkwater preferred to be forthright and to the point. There was nothing gained by mincing words. He sent the two men to kill Johnny Raybold in the same cold calculating way he might dispatch a broker to take up stock in a company he needed, or an accountant to check the books of a business he aimed to buy in on. So he expected to hear, without frills, the result of their mission.

'It didn't,' replied the taller man. 'Raybold's still alive.'

'*What?*'

'That's right. We jumped him at a good spot, threw down on him from behind and missed clean.'

The small eastern dude and the burly hired killer stood

97

facing each other. Their eyes locked for a moment, but it was the gunman who looked away first. He suddenly knew the small dude, a man he might at other times have despised as a coward who hired his fighting done, was more deadly and dangerous than himself. If Drinkwater hired his fighting done it was not from fear, but because such a way be more convenient.

'You mean you shot at him from long range?' Drinkwater snapped.

'Mister,' said the small gunman. 'That there was *Raybold*, Johnny Raybold of the Wedge. He's a handy boy in a fight and can throw a gun fast enough to make things *real* interesting. Happen we'd come riding in close at least one of us would still be out there.'

'What happened?' demanded Drinkwater, his voice throbbing with fury.

'Like we said,' replied the taller man. 'We threw lead at Raybold and missed. Then he pushed across the river and laid up behind a rock at the other side.'

'Yeah, got in a place where he'd take some moving,' agreed his pard. 'We took to the rocks at the other side. Tom here started to head upstream, saw a chance of tossing lead into Raybold from the side while Raybold watched me. Only it didn't work out that way. Somebody came up on the rim over Raybold's back, somebody who could handle a carbine real good. That was when we headed for the hills.'

'And came straight back here?'

'Look, mister,' growled the shorter man. 'We've maybe never been to no fancy eastern school but that don't mean we can't think straight. We rode a long route back and one that wouldn't be likely to be easy followed.'

'Good!' grunted Drinkwater.

'Yeah,' agreed the man. 'Real good. We started thinking on the way back, got to adding things up. Made us some sense.'

'Such as?' said Drinkwater warily, his instinct warning him of trouble ahead.

'Such as how you hired hard-cases like us to crew this fancy spread. It never hit us at first. Then we got it. Raybold was heading to the Rio Hondo country. The *Rio Hondo* country, mister. And you didn't want him to get

98

there. So Tom 'n' me got to figuring that whatever you needed us for had to do with the O.D. Connected.'

'And?' asked Drinkwater.

'We want out.'

The small man came to his feet in a fast move. He paced the room and looked out of the window. The ranch lay quiet, the guests dressing for dinner and in their rooms or cabins. He swung away from the window and returned to the men.

'So you want out?' he snapped.

'That and no more.'

'Bill Acre really picked some hard men, didn't he?'

If Drinkwater hoped to shame the men into staying on with him he failed. He could read no shame or anger at his words.

'He didn't hire idjuts,' replied the taller man. 'Which same he'd have to happen you want to make fuss for the O.D. Connected on their own land. We're getting out, mister.'

Suddenly Drinkwater found himself remembering Acre's warning words. The man had hired support without telling them what they would face at the other end. Now they knew and they wanted to get out as quickly as possible. However there were six more men on the spread, they offered him the nucleus of a fighting force and once others saw them standing they might join in.

'The rest of the boys feel the same way about it,' drawled the taller man.

'You told them?' Drinkwater growled, anger showing on his face, then going again for he had learned showing anger did no good and put him on a level with the men he hired.

'Some of 'em rode with us afore. They're friends. For the rest, waal, we don't none of us like being suckered into something like this.'

'All right. I'll pay you off.'

Defluer did not take such a calm view of the proceedings when he heard the news that evening.

The more important matter of how to stir up the Rio Hondo families against each other took precedence over all other business between the two New York financiers.

They discussed ideas, ways and means, but all needed men, men without scruples and who would be willing to

99

face up to the guns of the Rio Hondo bunch. Yet no such men could be found in Texas it seemed.

Finally Drinkwater, pacing the room like a restless cat, staring at the rain driving against the glass, blinking at lightning flashes which ripped the sky apart and scowling when thunder interrupted his thoughts, came to a halt before the table. He slammed an angry fist down on it.

'What is it about the O.D. Connected that makes men run like rabbits before them?' he asked, raising his voice in a strangled yell of pent-up fury. 'What is it about them. I wish to God I could see it!'

From outside came a rolling crash of thunder, a jagged and extra brilliant flash of lightning. It was as if some primeval, pagan god had heard Drinkwater's plea and gave a promissory sign that he aimed to do his best to set the scene whereby Drinkwater could see what made the Rio Hondo men so feared.

Joel Kent rode easily in his double girthed saddle, or as easily as a man could when wearing a dripping wet slicker and with water trickling down from his hat. He rode the O.D. Connected–Double B line, a dreary thankless task in this kind of weather but one which must be done. There was little to do, little to see and he looked forward to meeting Jackie Cormack and exchanging the gossip, telling how Johnny Raybold of the Wedge had taken to sparking with Betty Hardin. Only it might be some time before he ran across Jackie and until then Joel thought of his own position in life, of the other hands who would most likely be taking things easy back at the spread.

'Damn Texas in winter!' he said. 'Damn the rain! Damn everything! It's all Cap'n Dusty's fault I'm out here. He's picking on me because I set the boys to jump him a couple of days back.'

Although Joel knew full well there had been no unfair division of labour, or picking on him it made him feel better to believe he was the victim of his boss's spleen. He spent the next miserable half mile plotting various types of revenge on Dusty, varying from the impossible to the homicidal.

'Just you wait, boss,' he told the disinterested animal. 'One of these days I'll get that mean ole Cap'n Dusty and

I'll—whoa there! Trouble ahead.'

He saw a horse walking slowly along, a horse saddled, with reins dangling—and without a rider. Any time a horse came along with an empty saddle it gave grave cause for concern. Joel rode slowly forward, looking to the horse, crooning a low tune to soothe it.

'Easy now, ole hoss,' he said. 'Easy there now.'

Coming close he reached out a hand to the stray's reins, caught them and brought the animal to him. A cold feeling hit him as he looked down at the saddle, recognising it for what it was.

Joel wasted no time. Leading the stray horse he rode at an easy pace, but kept his eyes on the ground, reading tracks which had not yet become washed out. He topped a rim and saw Jackie lying sprawled out on the ground, saw other signs too which sent him forward at a faster speed.

Leaving the saddle Joel ran to his pard's side and dropped to one knee. He looked down at the youngster, seeing the open slicker, the half-drawn knife, the blue-black hole between the eyes, all the blood washed away from the wound. Joel could almost see what had happened. It showed in the guts, the half-cleared blood on the ground.

'Somebody's been slow-elking!' Joel growled.

Slow-elking in Texas meant hunting down and killing another man's beef either for private consumption or sale of hides and beef. As a crime it ranged along with rustling if the slow-elker sold the meat. The O.D. Connected might overlook a poor family travelling over their land and taking a steer for food. They would not overlook what looked like a piece of wholesale butchery.

For a moment Joel stood looking down. Then the message of the half-drawn knife hit Joel and he gave a low growl. Young Jackie's knife caused him to die. He must have come on the slow-elkers in action and, reckless to the end, pitched in to stop them. Only he went with his knife undrawn.

A low sound came to Joel's ears. He jerked erect, hand clawing at the front of the slicker to try and open it.

They sat their horses on the rim above him, half a dozen savage, vicious faced Mexicans, hats dripping water and serapes soaking wet around their shoulders. In the front of the party, afork a big, fine looking grulla stallion, sat a big, bulky man. From the silver decorated hat, through the fancy serape, the tight legged, flare-bottomed, charro trousers he spelled rich man, but the face looked even more evil than those of his comrades and they were no oil-paintings in the beauty line. In his hand he held a silver mounted Colt 1860 Army revolver rechambered for metal cartridges, it lined the muzzle down at Joel.

The gun roared, flame lashed from its barrel, lead struck Joel in the body and spun him around to crash on to his back. His small body arched once, then went limp.

'You shoot well, Tortilla,' said a small, rat-faced man who looked to have more than his fair share of Indian blood.

'Look him over,' replied the big man. 'I rarely miss. It is well to be sure. Ride down there, Robles.'

Riding forward the small man looked down. He threw a glance at the two horses which had jumped away at the sound of the shot. Then he looked down at Joel, seeing the hole over the left breast side of the slicker. No blood came through yet but that did not surprise the small man.

'He is finished,' Robles remarked with no more feeling, in fact less feeling than he would show if discussing the weather. 'How about the horses?'

'Leave them,' Tortilla replied. 'Take the meat on the pack ponies. We wait for the buyer at Phillipe's.'

'When does he come?' another man asked.

'Maybe tonight, or tomorrow morning. We have enough meat to supply him this time. By the time anybody finds these two there will be nothing to show how they came to die. Let's go.'

With that Tortilla turned his horse. It had taken some time to butcher out the steers and the men were just about to leave the area when they had heard Joel's horse approaching. Tortilla turned back to make sure no alarm could be spread. Now he rode away sure that he could not be tied in with the deaths of the two hands and that the rain would have washed out all signs of his passing long before the dead men were missed and a search started.

Time dragged by, the rain continued and the sounds of departing hooves faded away. Then slowly Joel sat up and looked around him. He opened the front of his slicker and removed a thick mail order catalogue the front of which had been ruptured and split by Tortilla's bullet, a bullet that had not passed through the thick stout paper.

'Fool for luck,' he said quietly. 'Ole Egbert'll be riled when he hears what happened to his dream book.'

Joel made for his horse, but the animal backed away, swinging its head, not running, but aiming not to be caught and ridden either. The cowhand snarled out a string of curses. He knew he would never catch the horse without the aid of a rope. This came close to being the worst kind of lousy luck a man could ask for, like he'd had his full share doled out when the bullet struck the dream book instead of his body. Yet the fool horse couldn't have picked a worse time to get ornery. He had to carry word to the home buildings, to get the crew out, have word passed to Hondo Fog and the Double B that they might move out, head for Phillipe's and land on the Mexicans foot, horse and artillery.

A low muffled snort came to Joel's ears and brought him around, hand fanning to his Colt. He thought one of the greasers might be back, in which case he aimed to go fighting.

What stood behind him was no Mexican—it was something a heaped-up sight more dangerous to a man afoot.

For a moment the longhorn bull studied Joel, raking up mud with a forepaw and blowing spray from its nostrils. Then it charged, came with head down and tail held erect and stiff.

Joel brought out his gun, throwing lead into the bull's face, thumbing off the shots as fast as he could. Even so the impetus of the charge carried the animal on at him. He threw himself to one side, slipping in the slick grass and sprawling down, the gun falling from his hand. He heard the meaty thud as the bull lit down, heard its dying moans and rolled over, catching up the Colt. If he needed the gun again before he cleaned it he was sure in bad trouble.

The bull lay sprawled down, all but dead. Joel came to his feet and growled as he saw another mark to be added to the growing list for which Tortilla must pay. Only Tortilla would not pay unless Joel could catch that fool hoss and burned shoe-iron for the O.D. Connected.

'Hey!' yelled a voice, the most welcome voice Joel could ever remember hearing. 'Hey there, why for all the shooting?'

'Sweeney!' Joel bellowed. 'Over this way and *pronto*!'

Hooves thundered as the lean, gaunt and miserable shape of Sweeney tore into sight. He rode for the Double B and had been Jackie's relief, out looking for the youngster. Now he'd found Jackie and he didn't like what he saw.

'Who did it, Joel?' he asked, the anger deep and bitter in his voice.

'Tortilla and his bunch. We've got a slow-elker at work.'

'Slow hell!' spat Sweeney, then he saw the hole in Joel's slicker and the ruined dream book. 'What happened?'

'I had some luck. Was bringing the dream book back from Jimmo for your fool old cook. Tortilla threw a .44 ball into me, only he hit the book and I stayed down until he pulled out. He's headed for Phillipe's place. Likely aims to stay on there, not knowing I'm still alive.'

'He'll stay there all right!' promised Sweeney, glancing at the dead bull and reading its brand. He also knew Joel had no choice but shoot for a longhorn feared man so long as he rode a horse. A man afoot stirred up all the hate a longhorn felt and near-on always brought a charge. Joel sure had been having things rough.

'Dab a loop on that hoss of mine,' Joel said. 'I'll help you load Jackie on his'n, then we'll make our spreads and turn out the boys.'

Without argument or further speech, without even a jeering comment on a man who let himself be caught afoot and lost his horse, Sweeney complied. He caught the horses and led them back to where Joel waited to lend a hand. Between them they hung the still, limp body across its saddle. Jackie was taking his last ride, he would never carry out his boast that one day he would show the Kid how to throw a knife.

'I'll get that ole Sharps gun off the wall,' Sweeney drawled, turning his horse, bringing Jackie's mount around also. 'Meet you in the woods back of Phillipe's place.'

'I'll be there,' promised Joel. 'Don't start in to taking them afore we all come in, Cap'n Fog wouldn't like that.'

He turned his horse and headed out across the range at a gallop. The horse, despite its other faults, was a mud-running fool, which was why he selected it from his string. Where other horses might flounder, slip and slide that line-back gelding kept its footing like a bighorn sheep scaling a crag face. Right now that mud-running skill counted for plenty, made Joel forget the horse's past behaviour. Only one thing mattered now. Getting to the O.D. Connected and the crew out to Phillipe's.

The sweating, lathered horse slid to a halt before the big house of the O.D. Connected. Joel left the saddle, lit down running to the bawling of the blue-tick hounds from indoors. He pulled open the front door without even knocking and entered. Dusty, Betty and the other members of the floating outfit came from the dining-room and towards him.

For once Betty didn't cut loose with a flow of hide-blistering at Joel for tracking mud into the house, or coming in dripping water. She knew the matter which brought him must be urgent or he would never have dared enter without knocking, or in such a state.

'Trouble, Cap'n Dusty!' Joel croaked.

Mark reached him first, helping him towards a chair while Betty drove off the hounds. She swung around and snapped: 'In the dining-room, Mark, get some hot coffee down him!'

'It's Tortilla!' Joel gasped out, as Mark started steering him to the dining-room. 'He's been slow-elking!'

'Get to the bunkhouse, boy!' Dusty ordered. 'I want every man saddled and ready to ride. Johnny, get out some ammunition for all the guns. Lon, take off for Polveroso, tell pappy to meet up with us either in Diggers, or back of Phillipe's place.'

In his wheelchair Ole Devil watched everything, nodding at the smooth way his segundo handled things. It had been the same in the war, given an emergency Dusty took command, handled things the way they should be handled.

While Joel slumped in a chair and revitalised himself with steaming hot coffee he told of the happenings out on the line. Gunbelts were strapped on, rifles taken from the case on the wall and loaded. By the time Dusty, Mark, Waco and Johnny collected their horses from the house stables the crew were saddled and waiting. There was no joking or cursing the rain as they sat in their slickers, already wet with the slackening rain. The men sat grim-faced and angry, their very silence boding no good for Tortilla and his bunch.

At the Double B, in the smaller, but comfortable ranch

house, Sweeney told his story to the three brothers and fortified himself with Sue's hot, black coffee. The girl's eyes went to her husband as he took the Spencer carbine from the wall and headed to where his gunbelt hung on a peg.

'Used to hunt coon and go fishing with Jackie,' Red said quietly.

'Now simmer down, lil brother!' Buck barked. 'You're a married man and——'

Sue swung around and walked straight to her brother-in-law, looking up into his face.

'Just what do you allow I am, Buck?' she asked, voice brittle and hard. 'My Red's as good a fighting man as you've got. Reckon I could look him in the face happen I stopped him going out to square things for his pard?'

'I thought——'

'Which same only goes to show,' Sue put in. 'You're too old to start thinking after all these years. Which same I'll make a right becoming widow-woman.'

Slinging his gunbelt around his waist Red let out a wail. 'Hear that. Only married for over a year and she allows I'll make a right nice corpse.'

'Cut that off, both of you!' Buck growled. 'It's not even starting to get funny.'

'Know something, big brother,' Red replied. 'You could be right at that. Go get a box of tubes, honey.'

Sue hurried away without another word. This would be the first time since their marriage that force of circumstances sent her husband out into possible danger. Yet she knew he would go along, that was the way of her man. Jackie had been a friend, she liked him, being reminded of Red in his ways. Now Jackie lay dead and the men who killed him must be punished. The girl had no sympathy with theories of reforming criminals, she knew how few such attempts succeeded. With men like Tortilla and his *bandidos* there could only be one kind of reformation—the kind handed out by a roaring gun.

'Know something, little gal,' drawled Buck gently after Red headed to the stables. 'You asked me that first night if I was satisfied with Red's choice. I said then I was—tonight's given me nothing to change my mind.'

'Thanks, Buck,' she replied. 'You take care of that man of mine.'

'Sure, little gal, sure. I'll tell Egbert to come on in with you until we get back.'

Red returned before the crew pulled out. He took the girl into his arms and kissed her. Sue clung to him, her little hands clamping on to his arms through the slickness of the yellow oilskin fish he wore. For a moment she did not speak, then looked up at him.

'Don't ride no bullet, Red honey.'

'I'll steer clear of them,' he replied. 'But this has to be done.'

'I know,' she said gently. 'Come back to me, Red boy.'

A few minutes after Sue stood at the doorway, ignoring the rain which spattered down on to her face she watched the crew riding out, led by Buck and Pete and taking her man with them.

The scene was set. The pagan god who answered Drinkwater's wish had provided the cast, laid on the place close at hand. Soon Drinkwater would know just what made the O.D. Connected men feared by their enemies.

CHAPTER TWELVE

PHILLIPE'S CANTINA

The night was dark, but the clouds whipped away for odd moments at a time allowing the full moon's light to illuminate the town of Diggers Wells and the men who gathered on its outer fringe. The rain no longer fell and the group of silent cowhands removed their slickers, lashed them to saddle cantles, then felt at the butts of their guns. From where they sat they could make out the glow of light at Phillipe's place and hear the noise from within.

Sitting side by side the three Blaze brothers were silent and thoughtful. Jackie rode for them from the day he left school, starting as wrangler and making a hand. They liked him, treated him almost as a younger brother. Now he lay dead in the Double B barn and the men who killed him sat whooping things up not more than half a mile away. Yet it would be worse than foolish to try and take the place without the aid of the O.D. Connected. Unless the cantina could be surrounded Tortilla might yet escape them.

'They're coming!' Pete said quietly, as if scared his voice might carry to the distant cantina and alarm its occupants.

Two men came from the darkness, both tall men. The huge white stallion and the black clothing identified one as the Ysabel Kid. The star on the other's jacket announced him to be Hondo Fog, sheriff of Rio Hondo County. Although his territory ended on the far side of the Rio Hondo, the sheriff still had authority to be here. Between himself and Sheriff Jack Packard of Teckman County existed something better than a gentleman's agreement. Each sheriff was marked on the other county's books as a deputy. In that way either could cross the county line after a fugitive.

Tortilla did not know this. Nor did he know how close his enemies were to snapping on his heels. Or that, right or wrong, permission or not, Hondo Fog would still have come after him.

'Any sign of the O.D. Connected?' asked Buck as the two men rode up.

''Bout a mile behind us,' replied the Kid. 'The sky'll be clear in an hour.'

'You want us to start moving in, Uncle Hondo?' Red inquired, knowing clear moonlight wouldn't help them any in the matter of surrounding Phillipe's.

'We'll wait for Dusty,' Hondo replied.

Soon after the O.D. Connected men rode up, mingling with the Double B crew while their leaders joined the sheriff's party.

'Do we move in now?' asked Red.

'We'll move in,' agreed Hondo.

'Hold hard,' drawled the Kid. 'Let me take off ahead as scout.'

The others saw the wisdom of the suggestion and Hondo gave his permission.

'I'll come with you, Lon,' Waco put in. 'This here's a two-handed chore.'

For a moment the Kid hesitated. He knew the dangers of the task ahead of him and didn't want to land the boy in something deeper than they might pull out from. Not that the Kid doubted Waco's ability to handle himself in any man's fight, just the opposite. It was merely that the Kid, like Dusty and Mark, felt an affection for Waco, treated him like a younger brother. A man didn't take to the notion of having his kid brother along when there stood a better than fair chance of not coming out of the game alive.

'What're you fixing to do, Lon?' asked Hondo Fog, knowing that black dressed, baby-faced hell-twister from way back and not fooled by his innocent looks.

'Go down there and bake up a mess of beans.'

That left a tolerable lot unexplained, even to men who knew *tortillas* went down very well with baked beans. It did not satisfy Hondo.

'Get that closer to the trail,' he ordered.

'We're going down there, look around, find out if there's guards out,' drawled the Kid. 'Then we're going inside to see what Tortilla and his men are loaded for, bear or squirrel.'

'You're going into Phillipe's?' growled Hondo, startled.

'Why sure, be better'n sneaking up and peeking through the windows even happen Phillipe cleaned them said windows off so a man could see through them.'

'Tortilla know you?' Dusty put in.

'Not from a long time. I was some youngster when I saw him last, then only for a spell and he doesn't know the boy at all.'

Waco gave a grin, it looked like he was cut in on the deal after all.

'Phillipe knows you,' Mark put in.

'I don't figure Phillipe's likely to get into the middle,' answered the Kid. 'He's got too much at stake in the game to cross either me or Tortilla, so he'll just see the bets and let 'em ride until he's certain sure which way to go. See, he knows that the minute he opens his mouth to call us down either me or the boy'll put lead between his two eyes, and that he doesn't want.'

None of the others spoke for a full sixty seconds after the Kid's last drawled word. All knew the dangers their two *amigos* would be moving into. Likely all of Tortilla's bunch would be inside, except the men left out on watch. That would be anywhere between ten and twenty against two, even counting the wide spread Lone Star belief that one white man was equal to two Mexicans, four if he be born in Texas. Only they needed to know what strength lay in the bar-room so as to know how to best set about fetching that same strength out again.

'Play it your way, Lon,' Dusty said quietly.

He did not ask his father to share the responsibility of sending two good friends into what might easily be their graves. Dusty accepted the decision as his own, made it without wanting other men to be in a spot where he could point and say: 'They helped me choose.'

'We'll go on down there,' drawled the Kid. 'When you hear the call of a whip-poor-will sound twice, start to ease the boys in and all around. Only make sure they know not to throw any lead at the first pair out happen any fuss starts. If we leave at all we'll be leaving fast.'

Dusty's hand clamped on Waco's shoulder. 'Mind you don't do anything foolish in there, boy. And if fuss starts light out fast.'

'I'll do that, pappy.'

'See you do, it's been a fair spell since Mark and me had to chap some sense into you.'

A grin split Waco's face. He had never been held down over a table and had a pair of bull-hide chaps applied in the manner of a schoolmaster's cane and he sure didn't aim to give Dusty and Mark cause to alter this.

'Let's ride, boy,' drawled the Kid. 'Mind what I said, you bunch. If you-all hear fuss in there wait until you're sure who comes out afore you throw lead.'

The hands rumbled in agreement. All knew just what risks Waco and the Kid took and those same risks wouldn't end when they got out of the cantina, especially if any of the circle of waiting men started to pour home lead without seeing who made a hurried departure from the building.

Swinging his huge white stallion the Kid started to ride away, Waco's paint moved in at his side, then Mark rode forward to join them. The Kid looked around and shook his head.

'Two's more'n enough in there at one go, Mark.'

'Which same I'm not fixing to go in,' Mark drawled in reply. 'I'll tend your horses for you and bring up the others once you're inside.'

'Smart thinking,' drawled the Kid.

'Bet Dusty thought of it,' went on Waco *sotto voce*.

'Bet I can tell you somebody who's due for a licking when this is over, too,' Mark answered.

Phillipe's cantina lay in the centre of a bosque, a large wood, about half a mile outside Diggers Wells. A long, low, one floor building most of which was taken up by a bar-room and kitchen. There were half a dozen small rooms along the corridor and facing the kitchen, back of the bar-room. They didn't offer much comfort, but Phillipe's roomers were not inclined to be fussy on such matters.

Few white men used the cantina, he drew his trade for the most part from a floating Mexican population. The odd *gringo* who came mostly drifted in after dark, paid his money, stayed the night, or a few days, then drifted on. There was no such formality as signing a register, or stating one's name and business. A man came, stayed and left without ever being noticed at all.

Despite the lateness of the hour Phillipe's place rang with

111

music, laughter and noise as the three Texans halted their horses among the trees, on the edge of a narrow path which led to the cantina. The Kid removed his spurs, drew his bowie knife and disappeared into the darkness. For fifteen minutes there was neither sight nor sound of him, then in the same silence he disappeared, the Kid returned.

'Nary a one outside,' he said. 'That's not like Tortilla.'

'Maybe allows he doesn't need lookouts, that we haven't heard about him killing Jackie yet,' Mark replied, hitting the nail clean on the head although he did not know it.

'Let's go, then,' drawled the Kid. 'See you, Mark.'

Standing before his horse Mark watched Waco and the Kid fade off along the path. He wanted to go along, but knew that would be foolish, dangerous and might ruin the entire mission.

The haunting cry of a whip-poor-will came twice. Mark swung around and mounted his horse and headed back to the main body. By this time Hondo had given them all their positions, warned them again not to shoot unless they knew what they shot at. He nodded and the men moved forward. They left their horses at the outer edge of the wood then started moving through the trees. The Kid's guess about weather conditions proved correct. High overhead the moon, after showing at odd intervals, now stayed in sight, lighting the area with cold, impersonal glow.

It took time, but the men split into their groups and headed through the trees. Hondo, Dusty and Mark faced the front doors, standing in cover. Buck's party moved in to line the horse-filled corral and Buck prepared to release the animals once the shooting started. Pete had charge of the rear, his men watchful and ready to prevent anyone leaving that way. Red held command of the left side, the red-head setting them out with quiet precision. Wild and reckless he might be, likely to hop feet-first and fists flying into any fight he saw, but once in the fight he became cool, calm, capable and so it was this night. At Red's side Sweeney cradled his .45 calibre Sharps Old Reliable rifle, fifty long bullets for it hanging heavy in the strap around his shoulders.

Still no sign of trouble from the cantina. Buck Blaze heard the rider and thought it might be one of the hands who straggled. He could have cursed the stupid fool for coming up on his horse in that way. Too late Buck saw the man pass, saw he wore a white shirt and string tie under his heavy greatcoat. The man had passed in beyond the circle of waiting cowhands and headed towards the front of the cantina. Buck growled silently. He did not dare risk calling to the man. In any case a visitor to Phillipe's at that hour most likely would be on the run from the law. A warning shout could bring a bullet in reply and warn Tortilla's men that all was far from well outside.

On the far side, before the cantina, Hondo Fog and his son cursed under his breath as they saw the rider turn the corner and halt before the front doors. They did not know how he came to pass through the other members of the party and Dusty swore he would level somebody's face if it had been through idleness or neglect.

Hondo's big hand clamped on Dusty's left arm.

'Hell fire, boy,' he said, watching the man open the door. 'Do you recognise him?'

Dusty nodded. He recognised the man. He also knew all hell was due to pop in a very few minutes.

Inside the cantina things were gay. A guitar player beat out a wild, stirring rhythm and a girl, one of the four Phillipe hired, danced on a table, her bare feet slapping out the beat, her sinuous body weaving and vibrating. At the table sat Tortilla, his serape gone and leaving exposed his heavy frame in all its silver filigree decorated magnificence. He watched the girl with drooling lips, thinking of pleasures to come.

The other three girls carried trays of drinks around, avoided or accepted the touches from grabbing hands, laughed, flung coarse jokes at the men and generally made themselves agreeable to their boss's customers.

Behind the bar Phillipe poured drinks with deft hands, grinned at the customers in his effort to show them his heart was in the right place and watched everything happening in the room. He looked up as the door opened, but the tobacco fumes and the general hazy atmosphere of the room prevented his getting a clear view of the new arrivals until they were halfway across the room. The guitar stopped playing, the girl's dance came to a stop, she stood on the table, legs braced apart, mouth hanging open just a trifle with the exertion of dancing, eyes studying the two

113

men who entered.

Every other eye in the room went to the newcomers. Waco often woke at night in time to come and found himself sweating, after dreaming of that crowd of hostile and evil looking faces. The men in that room looked just about as mean and ornery a bunch as he had ever seen. There might be a shred of humanity, decency or respect for human life among that lot but a man would have to dig hellish hard to find it.

The Kid also studied the room, studied it with the cold, impersonal eye of a man long used to Mexican border gangs. Not counting Phillipe's little bunch of employees, he made the herd tally twenty-three at least, which meant Tortilla had built up his band some. Not all were top-grade stock, but all looked like they'd be a sight safer when dead.

By now Phillipe could see his guests. See and recognise them. He knew the Ysabel Kid of old and had seen Waco around. The question now arose, should he tell Tortilla or should he hold his peace and see what came off?

He got an answer. The Kid's red blaze eyes held his own and Phillipe read a message which started the sweat pouring down his face even more than before. Go ahead, said the Kid's eyes, talk. Tell Tortilla who we are. Only the moment you open your mouth I'll close it with a round .44 ball.

To Tortilla's watching eyes the two *gringos* spelled trouble and danger. He had an uneasy thought that he ought to recognise that black dressed Tejano, only it had been many long years back and the man he thought of was said to be dead, at least he no longer rode the Rio Grande smuggling contraband.

A sign from his boss brought Robles erect. The small man started across the room, he moved on cat-like feet, graceful and fast, a hand near the hilt of the knife which never left his side.

'*Saludos, señores*,' he began, then continued in Spanish with a demand to be informed of their names.

Both the Kid and Waco spoke Spanish, Waco enough to get by and the Kid as fluently as any man in the room. They didn't aim to have that known yet.

'You just try talking English, *hombre*,' ordered the Kid.

'Wha' ees your nam'?' Robles replied, speaking just

114

about his entire stock of English in one go.

'I just don't see how the hell that comes to be your affair,' Waco drawled back.

Robles understood enough English even if he didn't speak it. His hand closed on the hilt of the knife—and released it again.

Just how it happened, just how a man could get his gun out so fast, not one of the watchers could say. About half a second after Robles made his first move towards the knife he looked down the barrel of Waco's right hand Colt and his ears were still aware of the click which warned him the hammer lay back ready to fall on a cap and turn lead loose.

'Easy, boy!' said the Kid urgently. 'We got grief enough without you riling this bunch on us.'

Tortilla spoke English well enough. He understood both the Kid's words and what he believed to be the meaning behind them. The two young Tejanos were on the run from the law, most likely because the tall blond boy drew and shot once too often. They certainly looked a hard pair, and gave every sign of being ready for any trouble which came their way. Tortilla had come north of his usual haunts to make money, not having his men shot down in private, profitless and unnecessary arguments with proddy American owlhoots.

'Robles!' he said. 'Leave them.'

The small man left without an argument, though he threw angry scowls towards Waco. Pushing back his chair Tortilla made a sign, the music started again and the girl resumed her dance. The *bandido* leader rose and walked towards the bar where Waco and the Kid leaned.

'I apologise for Robles, gentlemen,' he said, nodding to Phillipe who reached for a bottle.

'Keep your hands above the bar top!' growled the Kid, sounding mean as all hell and watching Phillipe.

'A wise precaution, *señor*,' remarked Tortilla. 'You seem to have been around more than a little.'

'Let's say we weren't neither of us born yesterday, or the day afore,' the Kid answered.

'I've seen you somewhere before, *señor*?'

'Likely, I've been there.'

'Where?'

'Somewhere.'

From the way he let out the last word the Kid considered that line of conversation now closed. Tortilla had good men at his back, but he didn't aim to push the two salty Tejanos any, they looked like they would push back fast and forcibly at any man who tried. So he took the easy way out. Throwing back his head he roared with laughter.

'You are making the funny,' he said, and bellowed forth another laugh. 'Now drink, *señores*. Is all on Tortilla, whom I am.'

With that Tortilla headed back to his table and the pleasure of watching the girl dance. After a few minutes she decided enough was plenty and came to a stop, then jumped down to flop on to Tortilla's knee and lock her arms around his neck.

'How long do we stay here, Tortilla?' asked Robles.

Forcing his head from the girl's thrust up face, Tortilla looked at the other man and grinned. They spoke Spanish and the two Tejanos did not show any sign of understanding.

'Until the man comes to pay for the meat. Then we take it where he wants it and after that look for more cattle.'

Although they gave no sign of understanding both the Kid and Waco knew every word spoken. They also knew that Joel had called things right. Tortilla had been behind the slow-elking and Jackie's death. Now he awaited the arrival of a man who would buy the meat.

Time ticked by. The Kid and Waco could guess that by now their friends had the place surrounded. So far Tortilla's men had no thought of their danger. The time had come to move on, get out while the going was good.

'How far to the border, barkeep?' asked the Kid.

'You are leaving, *señor*?' asked Tortilla, extracting himself from the girl's hot-lipped kisses for a moment.

'Sure, we want to be south of the line as soon as we can.'

'Then I wish you luck.'

At that moment the door started to open. The Kid and Waco exchanged glances. Nobody ought to be coming in and yet the door swung open and a shape loomed at it. A shape they both knew and who in the moment the door opened recognised them.

'What the——!' began the man, his hand lifting and

116

pointing at the two Texans. 'If this's a trick——'

'Waco!'

The Kid barked one word, all he needed to say. Waco flung himself to one side, his gun coming into his hands as he headed for the side door. At the same moment the Kid went forward, racing for the main entrance. The bar lights glinted on steel, shining steel of the bowie knife in his left hand, dull blued on the barrel of his Dragoon Colt in the right. A man came up, hand fanning at a gun butt. The old Colt boomed like a young cannon, its round, soft lead ball smashed into the man's chest and threw him off his feet, into a bunch of his *amigos* who planned to intervene but left it a mite too late.

From the corner of his eye Waco saw Robles rear up, knife sliding out. The young Texan's left hand Colt turned and roared, Robles went down, his knife dropping at his feet. Then Waco saw the side door, saw too its bolt lay closed. There would be no time to start fooling with the bolt, so Waco took the only way out. He swerved on the run, hearing lead slap by his head. Apparently one of the yelling, startled bunch had a gun out even if he didn't shoot too well. Ahead lay a window and Waco hurled at it, arms coming up to protect his head, holding the Stetson hat firmly in place. He hit the window, going through it, carrying glass, frame and sash with him.

'It's me!' he yelled as he lit down rolling on the ground outside.

'I was expecting maybe General Robert E. Lee?' yelled back Red's voice. 'Get those fingers off the triggers, you bunch!'

With long strides Waco raced across the open, swinging off out of the light and feeling the welcome shadows close in on him. He reached the trees and at the same moment a hideous scream, cut off into a low gurgle, came from the front of the cantina.

Waco started to turn but Red's hand caught his arm and held him.

'Quit it, you young fool!' Red snarled. 'I'll bust your head if you try and go back.'

'Damn it to hell, Red!' Waco hissed back. 'That might have been the Kid!'

'I know that!' Red's voice sounded low, vicious and

117

savage. 'But even if it was you can't do a damned thing.'

Confusion and pandemonium reigned in the cantina. Tortilla's bunch were all more or less under the influence of Phillipe's ripe old tequila and fuddled by the turn of events. Even Tortilla, most sober and dangerous of them all, found himself hampered and impeded by the terrified girl clinging to his neck and screaming fit to wake the devil.

The Kid raced across the room, making for the still half open door. Before him stood Manny Meyer, owner of a store in Teckman, holder of a contract to supply beef to the Army post outside city limits. Only it looked like he aimed to hold his purchase price down by buying stolen meat.

From their first meeting the Kid had never cared for Meyer and it had nothing to do with the other man's Hebraic extraction. With a father who had been an Irish-Kentuckian and a mother with Comanche and French-Creole blood the Kid could hardly set himself up over any man for his birth and would not. His dislike of Meyer stemmed from many things, including an unproved suspicion that the other man had been behind the selling of liquor which sparked off a bloody Kiowa reservation riot and cost several lives.

Right now Meyer half-heartedly blocked the Kid's way to freedom, a thing on a par, for danger, to standing between a starving grizzly bear and the only way out of a cave.

Meyer dropped his hand, shoving aside his coat and reaching for the butt of his gun. He hesitated as the Kid rushed nearer, then fell back a pace. The gun came out, but the knife licked across in a backhand slash as the Kid kicked open the door. He heard Meyer scream, felt the knife blade bite home, sink in, heard the scream die off in a hideous croaking and felt blood gush out over his hand. Then he passed through the door in a rolling dive. He had heard the window shatter behind him and Waco's yell. The boy looked to have got out safe which was all the Kid cared about.

Running as fast as he could the Kid made the trees, felt a hand grip his arm and haul him into the safety and cover of a tall tree. Mark looked at him, relief showing even in the shadowy shelter of the tree.

'You hit?' Mark asked.

118

'Nary a scratch.'

'The boy?'

'He went through the window over to the side there. After that I don't know,' replied the Kid.

A yell from the other side of the building, around Red's section, cut off any further speech making. Mark and the Kid knew that voice, knew it and felt the relief bounce through them.

'Mark! Dusty!' yelled Waco. 'Is Lon out safe?'

'Safe as I could be, boy!' called the Kid.

At that moment the door of the cantina slammed closed and lights started to go out. Tortilla didn't aim to give in without a fight, that was for sure.

Inside the cantina Tortilla had hurled the girl aside, too late to stop the two Tejanos leaving and making good their escape. He put life into the excited and yelling *bandidos*. One look told him Robles would never rise again, the man the Kid shot lay sprawled on top of a table, blood spurting and oozing as his life twitched away. Meyer sat by the door, his back to the wall, his unfired gun at his side, his head tilted back and under his chin lay a terrible gash which exposed flesh, the windpipe, almost to the bone. Blood gushed from the wound, his white shirt was white no longer.

Everything had happened so fast that Tortilla and his men could not co-ordinate their efforts for seconds after the abrupt departure of the Ysabel Kid and Waco.

'Out with the lights!' Tortilla yelled. 'Shut that door!'

Both orders were obeyed, light after light flickering out, men grabbing their weapons and heading for cover, some to the kitchen, others to the small side rooms. Behind the bar Phillipe stood and shuddered. How long would it take Tortilla to start thinking, and ask how come Phillipe had not recognised the two Texas men.

CHAPTER THIRTEEN

THE BATTLE OF PHILLIPE'S CANTINA

For a few moments after the Kid and Waco made their escape from the cantina and all the lights flickered out inside, nothing happened. Both inside and out the waiting men listened for the first hostile sound.

Hondo Fog had been a lawman for several years, more than he liked to remember. This was no new situation to him and he knew how to handle it. He had good men at his back, maybe as many on hand as had Tortilla inside and maybe even better with their guns.

Now the problem was how to get Tortilla and his men out of the cantina with as little loss of life as possible. Which meant a rush at the door was out, so was the thought of mass charge from all sides. At men hidden behind stout adobe walls that would be nothing less than suicide.

'Tortilla!' Hondo called.

'I am here, *señor*!' came the reply from inside.

'We've got you surrounded, light the lamps, then come out with your hands raised high.'

A cackle of laughter came back, derisive and wild. 'You come on in and get me, *hombre*.'

'We can do that, too!' Hondo answered. 'Buck!'

'I hear you, Uncle Hondo!'

'Turn their hosses loose!'

'Loose they are!'

Buck's reply anticipated the event by five minutes, it having taken him that long to inch around in the dark and throw open the log pole gate of the corral and dive for cover as lead ripped from the cantina towards him. His men knew what to do, they yelled, whooped, fired shots in the air and startled the corral horses out through the gates. In the confusion Buck made good his return to cover.

'Your hosses are gone, Tortilla!' Hondo called. 'It's only

a matter of time. Come on out!'

'NEVER!'

'How about your men?' countered Hondo and repeated the speech in Spanish.

He knew he would never make *bandidos* like that bunch surrender without a fight. Born in a land where *ley feuga*, the law of being shot while trying to escape even when not trying to escape, was standard practice among law enforcement officers, no Mexican *bandido* would give himself up while there was a cat in hell's chance of fighting clear.

'My men stand with me!' Tortilla answered. 'If you want us come and get us!'

There Hondo had it. He gave the men their chance to come out, now they must be shot out, fired upon until either they were dead or surrendered. Only Hondo wanted the firing to be controlled, not wild with lead flying every which way.

'Tell the boys to take time out to make sure of their cover, Dusty,' he ordered. 'And tell them I don't want any heroes. They'll stay under cover and shoot until I give the order to move in, which won't be while there's a chance of any of them taking lead.'

'Yo!' came Dusty's cavalryman answer.

Passing around the circle of men Dusty gave his orders, or his father's orders, for the way they would carry on the fight. He collected Waco on the way for the youngster preferred to be around the floating outfit's members unless urgent duty took him elsewhere. The word passed from man to man, soon all knew what they must do and all affirmed their intention and ability to do it.

Yet through the night there could be but little doing. Tortilla, like a wise general, looked to his position. Inside the cantina's adobe walls, reasonably safe from Winchester rifle bullets the cowhands rarely carried weapons of greater power than the .44.28 calibre model of 1866 or the .44.40 Model of 1873; his men faced danger only when exposed at a window. They had food in plenty, water or wine to last them for days—but ammunition would need careful nursing. They had only what rested in their belt loops, or the straps slung over their shoulders. So they must not waste any of it.

'Keep down!' he ordered. 'Don't start shooting until we

know how things look out there.'

All his life Tortilla had been an incurable optimist. He believed firmly that some divine power shielded him from the fate of lesser *bandidos*. It had been this belief which led him to lead his own band and pull audacious raids which somehow seemed to pay off. It led him north of the line, north of his usual haunts, to raid an area most owlhoots, Mexican or American, would have steered well clear of. Now he felt sure that it would take him out of this hole, that things might not be as bad as they seemed.

Dawn's arrival showed Tortilla he was right. Things weren't as bad as they seemed, they were a damned sight worse.

Hondo Fog had never risen above the rank of major in the Texas Light Cavalry but he also had the capabilities of a wise general. He gave the word that the men should pair up in their cover, one to sleep, the other to watch, turn about through the night and all to be awake when the first light of dawn showed. A fair percentage of the men had ridden in the Texas Light during the war and all knew how to take and obey orders.

The men, all of whom were used to sleeping where they could, all managed to get some sleep during the waiting hours and all were awake and alert at dawn.

The side door slid open slowly, inching away, first a tiny slit, then widening. Red Blaze watched this, he swung the Spencer carbine and lined it as a man stepped out. The man held a Winchester carbine and stepped forth warily, his face gaunt and wolf-savage in the cold half light of dawn.

'Hold it!' Red snapped.

Whipping up the carbine waist high the Mexican fired a single shot, but it ripped a chunk of wood from the tree behind which Red stood. The old Spencer boomed in reply and the man whirled around, crashed into the door, then slid down. His arrival in such a manner caused the men inside some worry for he blocked open the door. Already lead from Red's party began to pour in through the open door, slashing and tearing through the air even if it hit nothing. A man crawled along the wall, bent and grabbed the dying *bandido*'s hand, then dragged him bodily back into the room. At the other side another man slammed the door closed and lead drummed on, passing through but too

122

spent to do further damage.

Red's shot brought on a rapid volley from all around the building as both sides, keyed up by waiting, began to bombard the other's positions. Soon it would be light enough to see everything clearly and Hondo gave the order to hold fire until they might see what they shot at.

All around the building the Texans took up their positions with fight-wise eyes. Pete Blaze put his knowledge of the cantina to good use by scaling into the stout branches of a tree and sitting there, rifle held ready and able to cover a kitchen window, look into one of the bedrooms. He also, and more important from his point of view, could see over the low wall and to the flat top of the cantina with a trapdoor in the centre.

Shortly after the sporadic fighting brought on by Red, Pete saw the trapdoor inch up. He rested his Winchester on a limb and gave a low whistle which brought Johnny Raybold, who had been his pardner through the night, to the foot of the tree.

'They're coming!' Pete mouthed and Johnny's nod told he understood.

A man's head showed through the trapdoor, then he started to crawl out, a slim, savage looking half-breed holding a Sharps carbine. The door stayed up and a second man emerged, carrying a Le Mat rifle from the look of it.

Pete did not fire without warning, even though his position would be no insecure one if under fire from men on the roof top.

'Drop the ri——!'

He never reached the end of the third word. The Sharps carbine lashed up into a shooting position slightly ahead of the Le Mat and into its user Pete threw his first bullet. The man spun around and pitched forward, stumbling and reeling towards the edge of the low wall. A volley of shots ripped up into him and he crumpled forward over the edge.

Pete saw none of this for now he had troubles of his own. The second man made a flying dive, landing under the shelter of the low wall. Now Pete had trouble for he sat out there, exposed like a coon on a log and just waiting for a redbone hound to swim out and haul him off—only it wouldn't be a hound, it would be a bullet from that Le Mat rifle, the barrel of which was already inching out into view.

Down below Pete, alert and watchful, Johnny saw the rifle and read its message correctly. He rested his Winchester against the side of the tree and aimed with some care. Then he touched off a shot and saw dirt erupt from the wall an inch to the right. Without even thinking about what he did Johnny levered home another bullet and touched the trigger. This time his bullet struck the barrel of the Le Mat, throwing it into the air just as its user pressed the trigger. The bullet went into the air, the rifle spun from its user's grasp and he turned to dive headlong towards the open trapdoor.

He almost made it. Pete's rifle beat a tattoo, dirt spurts rising in line behind the man, inching up on him. One struck home, then another, even as the Mexican's head and shoulders passed over the lip of the trapdoor. Slowly the body slid on, going out of sight, falling down the ladder resting up to allow exit through the trap door. The trap collapsed as the man fell through and Pete breathed a sigh of relief. He did not believe there would be another attempt to use the roof as long as he could stay where he was.

'Watch those downstairs windows!' he ordered his party. 'I feel sort of exposed up this ways!'

Now shooting began in earnest. Caught like rats in a trap the *bandidos* aimed to either blast their way clear, or take as many of the Texans with them as they could when they finally went.

Out front of the building Hondo Fog had his party spread out. Flanking him were Dusty, Mark, the Kid and Waco, the first relied on his trusted Model 1873 carbine but the others each handled a Winchester rifle. In the Kid's hands, lining on an open window, rested a magnificent weapon, the 'One of a Thousand' Winchester he won at the Cochise County Fair* and with which he could perform shooting little less than miraculous. They sent shots into the room whenever a target offered itself to them and already one of Tortilla's men paid the price for allowing Mark Counter a clear shot at him.

At the moment the Kid was not firing. He did not believe in wasting lead and any time that rifle in his hand cracked he aimed to do some good with it. He saw Waco's bullets strike the wood and splinter holes in it and the germ of an

* Told in *Gun Wizard*, by J. T. Edson.

idea began to form in his mind.

For a moment the Kid listened to the sound of shots around the cantina. He heard the whiplash cracking of Winchester rifles, the different note of twenty-inch barrel carbines, he heard the bellow of Spencer .52 calibre carbines. Then he caught the sound he hoped for, the crashing bellow of Sweeney's heavy Sharps.

Waiting for a lull in the firing, then raising his voice, the Kid yelled, 'Sweeney! Hey, Sweeney, get round here, *pronto*!'

'I'll be right there!' Sweeney replied.

He did not come the most direct route, but cut back among the trees and tried to keep himself under cover for the Mexicans were throwing lead at anything that moved and talked Texan. So it came about that Sweeney approached the Kid from the rear, darting from tree to tree, his precious Sharps in his hands, having fired only two shots so far for he did not waste those long shells if he could help it. The gun had power enough to shoot clear through one of Phillipe's adobe walls, a table used as a barricade and a Mexican if one happened to be behind it, then pass out at the other side wall, but Sweeney only shot when he had something to shoot at. He didn't know what the Kid might have in mind but wanted to find out.

A Mexican saw the *gringo* darting forward and wondered what inspired such a foolish action. He was still pondering on the matter when his rifle cracked. Sweeney yelled, lead took him in the leg and dumped him down in clear view of the cantina front but his fighting man's instinct held the rifle clear of the muddy and still soggy ground.

In his attempt to finish Sweeney the Mexican stayed exposed too long. He sighted his rifle, but from behind the trees guns thundered. The Texans knew their pard's danger and poured lead at the front side, making sure none might take advantage of the easy offered target. The Kid's rifle lever seemed like a blur as he threw four shots at the man. Only the first would really have been necessary for it passed into the man's head and shattered the back out on leaving. Yet so close on the heels of the first shot did the others follow that three of them ripped home before the man's body fell and the fourth just missed the gory mass which slid from sight.

Risking death at the hands of the Mexicans, Mark Counter left his rifle and charged towards Sweeney. He heard lead sing around his ears, then bent and scooped the wounded man up in his arms. With long racing strides Mark headed for cover and only the rapid crashing rifles around him saved him from taking lead.

Lowering Sweeney to the ground Mark looked down at the leg. He grunted, from the look of things Sweeney would be off that leg for a spell, but the bone had not been touched. Mark knew something about first-aid and set to work, using Sweeney's bandana as a tourniquet. The Kid came slouching over and Sweeney looked up.

'What'd you want, Kid?' groaned the wounded man.

'Got the makings?'

'MAKINGS!' Sweeney forgot the agony in his leg and raised the word in a combined rage and pain-filled howl. 'Makings! You mean you fetched me all this way, got me pumped full of lead, just 'cause you want a smoke?'

'Huh!' grunted the Kid. 'Happen I'd known you'd act that ways I'd've borrowed the boy's. Still, while you're out this way I'll take your rifle instead.'

'Rifle?' growled Sweeney suspiciously. Under normal conditions the Kid wouldn't even give a Sharps credit for being a good walking cane.

'Sure, and that belt of shells,' drawled the Kid.

Not knowing why the Kid wanted his prized long rifle, Sweeney still handed it over. Then Mark eased the bullet belt from around Sweeney's shoulders and passed it to the Kid who extracted a bullet and looked at it, weighed it in his hand and threw another look at the door.

'Got a knife?' he asked.

'Don't want my pants as well?' growled Sweeney, fumbling in his pocket and taking out a big folding jack-knife.

The Kid accepted the knife and opened its blade. Then he held the bullet and cut a cross-shaped groove into the lead nose. He repeated this process with about half a dozen bullets before Sweeney saw what he was doing and also remembered the bowie knife which never left the Kid's side.

'What in hell's name!' he howled indignantly. 'You've got a knife of your own without spoiling mine!'

'Sure, but I don't want to spoil mine's edge,' answered

the Kid calmly, then threw a look at the woods behind him. 'Folks coming, Mark.'

'Who?'

'Walk like townsmen. Be somebody out from Diggers most likely.'

A few moments later the men appeared, several citizens of the town, including the doctor, Mark was pleased to see. He explained quickly what had happened and the citizens offered to lend a hand while Mark gratefully handed over the wounded man to the doctor's care and followed the Kid back to the firing line.

'What're you fixing in to do?' Mark asked, watching the Kid stuff one of the prepared bullets into the breech of the rifle.

'I'm not sure yet,' admitted the Kid. 'It's just a fool notion.'

With that he aimed and fired at the door, sending the bullet into the centre of one of the planks. The rifle's bullets were known as .45/120/550, which transplanted into lay terms meant it propelled a five hundred and fifty grain bullet .45 in calibre, by the explosive force of one hundred and twenty grains of prime Du Pont powder. The bullet passed forth from the barrel at around a speed of fourteen hundred feet per second, developing up to two thousand three hundred pounds pressure per square foot on leaving the barrel, which was a tolerable amount of pressure. The split nosed bullet hurled out with all that powder and barely dropped any of it when reaching the door. Normally even a lead bullet would have passed through the timber like it was not even there. Only this time the bullet's nose had a cross cut into it and mushroomed out. The result looked real spectacular, a gaping hole ripped through the plank.

'Now see what you done!' Waco grunted, having watched the proceedings. 'Keep that fool game up and you'll bust a panel out.'

'Do tell!' replied the Kid. 'I thought I was making a hole so they could relieve themselves through it and save going to the backhouse.'

'Hole'd be too high,' drawled Waco. 'Unless those *hombres* have their'n set on higher than we do. Or maybe you reckon they like doing it standing on a chair?'

The Kid did not reply, but sent another bullet smashing home close to the first and another jagged tear appeared. On the third shot booming out the Kid had response from two sides.

'Kid, you danged Comanche!' howled Sweeney. 'I have to buy them shells, not you!'

'Why sure,' came the Kid's imperturbably cool reply. 'Which same is why I borrowed your fool g——!'

His speech ended as a close passing rifle bullet struck the tree behind which he hid and showered his hat with splinters. The Kid cursed. He was not annoyed at being shot at, in fact would have been worried had his efforts been ignored. However the rifle user, hidden behind a tipped up table which formed a barricade in one of the shattered window frames, impeded his task of opening the door in his own manner. He threw a look to where Dusty and Mark watched his efforts.

'Happen it wouldn't be too much trouble,' he drawled. 'I'd surely admire for you gents to stop that fool *hombre* blowing my head off while I'm working.'

'You only had to ask,' replied Dusty.

Only it would be easier said than done to remove that *hombre*, for he had a fairly good position. He also moved lively, going from side to side of the table and throwing a shot when he reached the end. Fast taken or not those shots served to hold the Kid down, preventing him taking the steady aim required to carry out his purpose.

Dusty lined his carbine and touched off a shot, splintering the side of the table. The man jerked back a pace or so and Dusty nodded. He loaded his carbine and looked at Mark.

'Pump lead into that table, move it along and keep him going.'

The big Texan needed no further explanation. His rifle started to crash out and at each shot a hole jumped in the table's face, moving from left to right. Nearer the end of the table the holes crept. Dusty's carbine lined, sights set on his prospective target. The other men out front guessed at the serious nature of the work and poured fire into the other front window to prevent any chance of it being interrupted.

Another bullet struck the table and the Mexican stepped back—too far. The carbine spat in Dusty's hands, just once, but the man spun around and crashed out of sight in that limp, boned-looking way a head-shot body always fell.

Even before this happened the Kid continued his lead throwing. Sweeney no longer complained for he saw the use to which his prized Sharps was being put. The Kid's next shot split the panel, opening up long cracks. He reloaded and threw yet another shell into the next panel. Sweeney, ignoring the doctor's orders, insisted on being brought up close and using his jack-knife to X-notch more bullets ready.

Hondo Fog joined his son and they watched the second panel splitting. Both knew full well what would soon happen.

'They'll be bursting out soon,' Hondo stated.

'Sure as eggs,' drawled Dusty in reply, then raised his voice. 'Pass the word to be ready for a rush.'

'And keep down, don't be heroes when they come out!' Hondo went on.

Inside the cantina's bar-room men watched the door being shattered by that pounding lead which came driving through, throwing huge splinters ahead of it. A man yelled something, none of the others were sure what. All knew that the door must soon collapse and leave them exposed to the Texans' rifles.

'Run!' Tortilla screamed. 'Rush them!'

From every window, from the back doors, they burst. Running men holding weapons and shooting as they came. They meant to shoot their way clear, escape if they could. Kill as many of their enemies if they could not.

But around the house lay a full twenty yards of open land, swept by rifle fire from men who could call their shots accurately. Tortilla's gang were ripped down, cut from their feet. Some threw away their guns and surrendered. Others held their guns and fired back until lead smashed them down and ended their lives.

In the last few moments, in the last dying embers of Tortilla's gang, the Texans suffered their most casualties. Three men were wounded, another killed and the man who tried to stir up trouble against the Lazy J the day Gus Gallom died, he went under too, victim of his own stupidity. Trying to impress the others he left cover to shoot down a wounded Mexican. The Mexican's last act alive was to raise his Colt and put a bullet into the Diggers Wells hard-case's head.

Tortilla had not come out yet. Dusty Fog dropped his carbine and raced across the open, his matched guns in his hands. He reached the shattered door and went through it fast. He came just in time to save Phillipe's life.

Just before the last rush, with the last shot sent home by the Kid into the door, Tortilla took lead. He knelt on the floor, but not in prayer. His gun lined on the terrified shape of Phillipe who cowered behind the bullet-pocked bar.

'You—you knew them——!' gasped Tortilla, realisation coming at long last. 'You knew the *gringos* and didn't say a word. I kill——'

'Tortilla!'

Dusty yelled the word and the *bandido* twisted, his gun roaring. The bullet stirred the brim of Dusty's Stetson in passing, then Dusty shot back and Tortilla rocked almost erect, stood for a moment and collapsed in a heap.

At the same moment Waco came in, throwing a bullet into a wounded man who reeled through the kitchen door and threw down on Dusty.

After that all fell silent. The awful silence which always seemed to come when the guns stopped their roaring and only the cleaning up remained.

Holstering his guns Dusty walked from the shattered bar-room. His father came forward.

'All of them?' he asked.

'Every last one,' Dusty answered.

'Go borrow a wagon,' Hondo ordered. 'Take the wounded and young Joel home. He took lead, finished.'

'Any more?'

'Dawkins from Diggers. We came off light,' Hondo replied, knowing Joel had been a good friend. 'Go on, boy. Leave Mark, Waco and Lon, take the rest home.'

Dusty left the room and called the cowhands around him. He told them what his father said. They did not argue. There was no levity as they walked back to collect their horses.

'You sure we couldn't help Uncle Hondo?' Red asked.

'He's got all the help he needs,' Dusty replied. 'And Sue's waiting for you. Get home to her, Cousin Red.'

CHAPTER FOURTEEN

THE POWER OF A BEAUTIFUL WOMAN

Drinkwater rode slowly towards the Lazy J after visiting the town of Diggers Wells. He rode in escorted by one of the cowhands early that morning, or what classed as early to a man raised on Eastern big business ideas. In town, while hoping to learn something of his enemies, or rather his potential enemies, he heard plenty of them. The details of the battle at Phillipe's were recounted to him with bated breath and in detail by a group of men at Big Ethel's saloon.

After hearing the story Drinkwater requested that he be taken to see the site of the battle and found his guide could take him out to Phillipe's. He found Sheriffs Packard and Hondo Fog still present although the bodies were taken away and the earlier sight-seeing citizens departed to Big Ethel's where they would discuss the battle and fight it over again.

It came as a surprise to Drinkwater when the cowhand introduced him as the boss of the Lazy J. He did not know the cowhand's almost inborn sense of picking out a real leader of men. Packard and Hondo greeted Drinkwater, asked him to look around inside, then keep his people away from the place for a few days until the worst of the mess was cleared up.

'It's not pretty even now,' Hondo Fog remarked, leading the way into the bar-room.

Drinkwater had never seen violence, or sudden death, nor had he ever seen the aftermath of a gun battle. Now he did and the sight hit him with its raw savage impact.

The room was a wreck, tables broken and bullet-holed, the walls drilled and punctured where lead smashed through, the window shattered, frames as well as glass gone. The bar had been raked by lead, broken tequila and other drink bottles long since dripped empty, but pouring forth the raw fumes of their spilled contents. The stench of the room was horrible, raw liquor, burned powder's acrid bite, and above it all the smell of blood. Men died in that room, shedding their blood on the uneven floorboards, and in one place not only blood, but the dull grey pulp of brains lay there.

'Let's get you out of here!' Hondo drawled.

He escorted Drinkwater from the room for the eastern man's legs did not seem to obey the dictates of his mind. Outside, on the hard packed earth between the house and the woods, he saw other dull reddish brown patches, blood shed by men who tried to fight their way clear and died in the trying.

It took Drinkwater some minutes, but he shook the revulsion from him. This would be no sight for his visitors to see, even as Hondo Fog warned it would not. Once over his shock Drinkwater spoke with Hondo Fog, wanting to gauge the other man's ability. Much to his surprise he found Hondo to be cultured, educated, a man of considerable intelligence and knowledge of the world, not some ignorant country bumpkin who held post of sheriff through kinship with the county commissioners. Drinkwater found himself revising many of his preconceived ideas. He no longer felt assured of the success of plans laid in far-off New York.

The battle at Phillipe's gave him a clear sign of how the Rio Hondo men could fight. The wrecked building, the bloodstains around it, they all bore mute testimony to the fighting prowess of the men he meant to drive from their homes. He thought over the details of the fight. How one of the most dangerous gangs of Mexican *bandidos* raided the Rio Hondo and killed one of their men. Then, not twenty-four hours later, the posse under Hondo Fog located and wiped the gang from the face of the earth, killing or capturing every last one of them for the cost of two dead and three wounded.

Discounting the luck in finding Tortilla so quickly, it still took fighting men to bring off such a coup.

With that thought in mind Drinkwater left the others and headed back to the Lazy J. He rode to town in the first place meaning to send a telegraph message to his man in Chicago, ordering that the toughs be brought down. Now he could see it would take something more potent than the brass-knuckles and occasional gun of the city toughs to handle the men of the Rio Hondo, so he did not send the message.

'You have visitors, sir,' said the ranch's manager when Drinkwater left his horse in the hands of his guide and walked towards the house. 'Mr. Defluer took them to your room.'

'And where is Miss Defluer?'

'She seemed a little put out that you didn't take her with you, sir, and has gone with the party to see the cowhands handle a herd.'

'Who are the visitors?'

By this time they were at the door of the main house and Defluer waited. So the manager fell back, not wishing to hear something not intended for his ears.

'Acre's here,' Defluer said, looking puzzled. 'With a woman.'

From the tone of Defluer's voice this was no ordinary woman. Drinkwater asked no questions, but entered the room. Acre stood by a side table and Drinkwater nodded to him, then looked at the woman who lounged with feline grace in a chair.

Without a doubt she was the most beautiful woman Drinkwater had ever seen. Her features seemed almost too perfect to be true and her figure warm, ripe, faultless. And a brain as cold, calculating and pitiless as an adding machine.

'Hello, Marie,' he greeted, with no hint of friendliness in his voice.

She came to her feet and walked towards him, smiling, yet the smile never touched her eyes. She held out a jewelled hand to him and he took it.

'Basil,' she greeted. 'You take some finding.'

'She said she knew you, Boss, wanted to see you,' Acre remarked. 'I allowed it'd be best to bring her over here myself.'

From Acre's tone there had been more to it than just that. Drinkwater knew Marie Rambeau from way back and knew hints of blackmail and blackmail itself were not the least of her talents.

'What do you want, Marie?' Drinkwater asked.

'I heard something of what you plan to do down here,'

she replied.

'Not from me, Boss!' Acre put in.

'Not from him. I was in Uvalde and heard of how the ranches were bought by an eastern man who sounded remarkably like my dear friend, Basil Drinkwater,' the woman replied. 'I cultivated the man who told me. Learned that the same man was now in Texas again, but in another town. I thought I would come along and pay my respects. This man of yours,' she waved a hand towards Acre, 'is very loyal. It took some persuading before he would bring me along.'

'You did the right thing, Bill,' Drinkwater remarked. 'Would you wait outside, Marie?'

'Of course,' she replied. 'I want money, Basil.'

'I never knew you when you didn't,' he answered.

She swept across the room and halted at the door. 'Basil, my sweet,' she said. 'Don't get any ideas. I have a friend who knows where I am and who is a most unpleasant young man when roused.'

To give credit where it be due Drinkwater had no such plans as removing Marie Rambeau from the face of the earth, at least not until she served him a very useful purpose. In fact he was most pleased to see the woman. She looked older, not quite so innocently naïve as when he last made use of her services, yet such beauty would dazzle the eyes of the men in these parts, while her wit and charm, she could turn on both like a bartender turning a tap in a beer barrel, would captivate the cowhands. She might have been sent by providence instead of coming with the express intention of blackmailing him.

'We've got it at last!' he told the other two. 'The splitting wedge. The Delilah who will shear the hair of the Rio Hondo Samson.'

Acre looked puzzled. 'Who's this here Samson, Boss?' he asked. 'I never heard tell of him working for Ole Devil Hardin.'

'The world doesn't begin and end at the borders of Rio Hondo County, Bill,' smiled Drinkwater. 'Samson was a legendary strong man in the Bible. He could not be defeated until Delilah cut his hair.'

'How'd that help?' Acre inquired.

'According to the legend his strength was in his hair,'

134

Defluer put in, a superior smile on his face.

'Yeah,' drawled Acre dryly. 'Well, don't let that fool you, bald as a billiard ball or hairy as old Jim Bridger, Dusty Fog's strength'd be the same.'

'He is rather hairy from all I've heard,' Defluer mused.

'Him?' grunted Acre. 'Dusty Fog? He's always been clean shaven when I've seen him.'

'You've seen him?' Defluer showed interest in the way he spoke.

'Sure. First time I walked right by him in the street and never gave him a second glance. A short, insignificant cowhand—then I saw him face down a drunken hard-case and I never thought of him as small any more.'

'You mean he's a small man, not big and black bearded?' croaked Defluer.

'Why sure, only there's not many think of him as small after the first time.'

Drinkwater scowled. He did not wish the business at hand to be carried into a discussion on the man who killed Defluer's son in the war.

'The thing is,' he put in, speaking in a manner which warned Defluer to get down to serious business, 'we have a chance to split the Rio Hondo men apart. You know how touchy about their honour these southerners are. The one thing which would set them to quarrelling would be a woman like Marie Rambeau.'

'That woman?' gasped Defluer, throwing a look at the door.

'*That* woman, my dear Aristes, is the one who came between the Bois-Fontaine brothers, caused them to fight a duel in which both received fatal injuries. She could split the Rio Hondo into feuding groups. Weaken them. Then we strike.'

'Would she do it?'

'For money she'd set her grandmother to cutting her mother's throat,' answered Drinkwater in calm assurance.

'Try her then,' Defluer suggested.

Crossing the room Drinkwater pulled open the door, catching Marie bending in a listening attitude. She showed no embarrassment at being caught in such an unlady-like act and yawned in his face.

'The room's sound-proof,' he told her. 'Come in, Marie.'

He took her across the room and seated her at the table. 'Can you do a job for me?'

'How much?' she asked coolly.

'It would be worth perhaps three hundred dollars,' Defluer answered.

She laughed, a musical tinkle that had no humour in it. Her eyes went first to Drinkwater, then examined Defluer with mocking disgust.

'What does your friend think I am, Basil,' she asked. 'If that is his idea of the value of the job, or the type of price it costs, you had better get some slut from a dance hall.'

Drinkwater could have cursed his friend. Now it would cost a whole lot more to hire Marie than if he had handled the affair without Defluer's help.

'We'll start with a thousand,' he said. 'Any more after that depends on your success.'

'Tell me what you want done. Is there some stupid young fool who knows of a business merger and you require the details?'

'Not this time,' answered Drinkwater, for she had served him in such a capacity before. 'I want trouble stirred up among some men. I want them setting at each other's throats. I want it doing as quickly as possible.'

'Lead me to them,' she replied. 'Who are they?'

'The leading members of the Rio Hondo country clan.'

'Cowhands?' she asked. 'My dear Basil, what could be easier.'

'For you, nothing, I'd say,' he answered. 'There's only one thing, Marie. These men don't exchange cards, call seconds and meet at dawn. When they fight it is done on the spot. They just draw and shoot.'

Her nostrils quivered a little and she started to smile. 'That will be most interesting. I have never seen a duel yet. Now, the names of the men you want removing and how much the job is worth altogether.'

The sordid details of business were soon settled. It did not come cheaply, talent of any kind never does. At last all was settled and Marie asked for an escort she could rely on to give her the first chance of meeting one of the men she must work against.

'I know most of them, Boss,' Acre said. 'And you don't want any of the other hands working on the spread to know what's going on.'

'Go ahead then,' replied Drinkwater. 'I've heard of the Turkey Shoot Ole Devil Hardin has next Saturday. If Marie can make contact by then she ought to be able to rouse something when all the men get together.'

A woman's scream brought Buck Blaze swinging around in his saddle as he rode across the range making for the O.D. Connected house to see his Uncle Devil and Cousin Dusty on a matter of business.

Behind him lay the Rio Hondo woods and from them a horse, bearing a scared looking woman, came running, going wild from the look of it. She clung to the saddle and clearly appeared to be unable to handle the racing animal.

Buck wasted no time. He put the Kelly spurs to work and the horse he rode went from a steady trot to a fast gallop in four swift strides. Heading his big roan at a tangent to meet the other animal, Buck studied the woman. He saw a beautiful face, a small hat set on dark hair, a trim eye-catching figure in an eastern riding habit of a pattern he'd only seen in newspaper photographs. He also recognised the horse, a bay sold by his uncle to the manager of the dude ranch as being steady enough not to spook or run wild when ridden by some leisurely eastern dude who had not tangled with western horse-flesh before.

The horses closed together. Buck's big roan had the legs of any saddle plug and came alongside the bay. Then Buck bent, scooping up the trailing reins into his hand, turning his horse by knee pressure alone. He brought both horses to a halt and jumped down.

'Easy there, hoss,' he said. 'Take it easy now.'

Then he turned and looked up at the woman's face. It looked flushed and yet not exactly frightened.

'Could you help me down, please?' Marie asked.

To her amazement Buck neither blushed, stammered incoherently, nor fumbled as he reached up and helped her from the saddle. He set her on her feet, released her and moved back, looking at the horse.

'Did he scare you?' he asked.

'A little. I knew I would be rescued though,' she replied and saw his brows draw together in a puzzled expression. 'That's always the way it happens in Ned Buntline's books,

137

you know.'

'I know,' he admitted, hoping none of his friends ever heard the confession. 'I've read some of them. Only I wouldn't rely on it in real life. It's only luck that anybody was out this way at all. Why'd he run?'

'I—I'm not sure.'

Buck's eyes went to the mark on the horse's rump. Something thin, a quirt most likely, had landed hard there. It would need to land hard to make that horse take to running scared as it had been.

'It may have been when I hit him to make him take a jump,' she went on.

Her explanation did not quite satisfy Buck. From the look of the weal it had been struck from somebody behind the horse. He did not express his doubts but just grunted: 'Fool trick that, ma'am. Could have got you hurt bad.'

With that he turned and walked back towards his horse. Marie watched him, her eyes narrowing slightly in surprise and annoyance. When she spoke she made her voice small, frightened and yet somehow promising.

'I'm afraid I'm hopelessly lost. Could you take me back to the Lazy J?'

'Lazy J, huh?' drawled Buck. 'You sure are lost. I'll head you in to Diggers Wells and that agent *hombre* will see you get back safe.'

After helping Marie to mount her horse Buck went back to his roan. He hit the saddle in a lithe bound and wondered what her motives might be. Of course she could be a rich young dude woman wanting a thrill. But why take the risk of the runaway horse to get to know him. A simple ride from the wood could have produced the same result with much less trouble. That slash with a quirt which started the horse running looked to have been struck by somebody behind the horse, the same somebody might even now be watching everything. It could be a version of the old badger game, but Buck doubted that.

'Been here long?' he asked.

'A day or so,' she replied. 'I'm from Boston. My name is Marie Rambeau.'

'The name's Blaze, Buck Blaze,' he replied, thinking she did not sound like any Bostonian he ever met.

'I'm pleased to meet you, Buck,' she said. 'May I call you Buck. You must call me Marie.'

For all that Marie felt confused. She'd seen cowhands in town, seen the way they ogled her and any other pretty woman who passed. Seen too the shy, awkward way the cowhand acted when faced with a pretty woman. Yet this man appeared to treat her as if she was just a part of the scenery, or a chance met stranger.

A wild yell came to her ears. She turned, as did Buck, seeing two young women and five men riding towards them. A frown came to her face, for it looked as if Buck did not exactly object to the diversion. He studied the riders and the eight hounds which loped by the horses, a grin came to his lips.

Marie studied the two young women, being unpleasantly aware that both were exceptionally beautiful and shapely. They returned her looks with frank interest and curiosity, but not with the animosity she had long been used to seeing on the faces of other women. Then she looked at the men, hardly noticing the small, insignificant cowhand on the huge paint stallion, but guessing some of the others might be the men she must work her evil charm upon and stir into quarrelling enemies.

'Where're your bunch headed?' he asked, seeing Hondo Fog's four brindle coloured Plott hounds and Betty's blueticks and guessing the answer.

'We aim to fix that old black bear's wagon for good this time,' the dark-haired girl replied. 'Don't we, Johnny?'

'Sure do,' agreed Johnny Raybold. 'Poor fool ole Mark got caught to handle the spread and the rest of us took off.'

While Buck Blaze did not mind a mild flirtation, even with the attendant risk of being watched by whoever started Marie's horse running, there was one thing he would much rather do, trail a pack of fighting hounds when they ran ahead and in full cry. He read the curiosity in Betty and the others' glances and turned to the woman by his side. Buck introduced her and confirmed her suspicions that these were the men she must work upon although she felt surprised that this small man could be the famous Dusty Fog.

'This's Miss Marie Rambeau, from Boston,' he finished.

Somehow Marie got the idea, after saying a few words, that these people knew Bostonian accents for they threw looks at Buck. Then Betty remarked they had better get on their way if they hoped to pick up the bear's trails this side of Christmas.

'You bunch don't know anything about working hounds after bear,' Buck drawled. 'I'll come along.' He turned to Marie. 'Top of that hill there you'll see a trail, turn left on it and follow it, you'll soon be in Diggers Wells and your own folks'll pick you up.'

'We'd ask you along,' Betty went on. 'Only you're not dressed for our style hunting. It gets rough up there in the woods when a bear starts to running.'

Never, in all the years she used her beauty to ensnare and betray men, had Marie felt such an utter failure. She watched the others turn their horses and headed towards the woods. Hate boiled up inside her. They would pay for that slight. Buck Blaze, all of them would know the fury of Marie Rambeau scorned.

Turning the horse she headed for the top of the slope, saw the trail and rode down to it. She had almost reached the Rio Hondo ford when Bill Acre rode out of the woods to join her.

'You sure did well,' he drawled. 'And don't get high-hand with me. I'm not over fond of your sort.'

He had doubted the success of the scheme from the start. Buck Blaze's apparent indifference to Marie's charms confirmed this. He watched the entire affair. Marie insisted a dramatic rescue would be the best plan, it took a hard whack from his quirt to start the horse running. At first Acre thought the meeting might bring some result. He did not think so any longer.

They reached Diggers Wells and Marie left Acre, heading for the telegraph office to send a message to a good friend. With this done she turned and walked out of the stuffy room. On the street she halted in her tracks, looking across to where Buck Blaze walked along the sidewalk. Buck Blaze and a pretty brunette girl wearing a gingham dress which went out of style three years before. When he saw the contrast between the girl and the more beautiful and worldly Marie Rambeau he would probably be easily won over. Then the girl would complain to her kin and trouble

140

would be on its way.

Marie crossed the street, coming on to the other sidewalk ahead of the couple, smiling a greeting. Yet Buck did not appear to recognise her. He did appear to have found time to change his clothes and now wore a green shirt and blue jeans instead of a dark blue shirt and levis.

'Why, Buck,' she said in her most seductive manner, watching the girl all the time. 'Surely you haven't forgotten our little adventure so soon?'

The man she thought to be Buck Blaze halted, swept off his hat and grinned.

'Danged if I don't grow a moustache,' he said. 'There's some mistake, ma'am.'

'But surely you and I met out on the range?'

'You've got your reins twisted, honey,' drawled the girl. 'This's Pete, not Buck. Look some alike though, I've been told.'

At that moment Marie remembered the Blaze twins. She felt like a fool. It was obvious Buck could not have beaten her to town and changed his clothes. She managed a smile she did not feel.

'I am sorry,' she purred. 'But the resemblance is remarkable.'

'I'm the youngest and best looking,' Pete grinned. 'What's Buck been up to, ma'am.'

'He rescued me when my horse ran away.'

'That makes a change,' smiled the girl at Pete's side. 'It's usually the girl who needs rescuing from Buck.'

'He hardly seemed dangerous. Why, he deserted me when some of his friends came along, going hunting.'

Pete and the girl laughed. It was the girl who replied. 'Honey, you're not the first and likely won't be the last. Those fool Blaze boys would rather hunt a pack of hounds than eat a meal. This one was as bad as the others, but I done got him house-broke.'

'Tell you though, ma'am,' Pete went on. 'You come over to the big house for the Turkey Shoot, you'll see Brother Buck some different then. Waal, come on, honey, let's get our chores done and head for home.'

Marie watched them walk off and her eyes flashed hate.

'Don't worry,' she hissed, speaking so they could not hear her. 'I'll be there all right. Then we'll see who has the last

141

laugh.'

She headed for where her horse stood before the Lazy J's town office. On Saturday she would go along to this Turkey Shoot and she would show the Rio Hondo bunch the power of a beautiful woman who had been scorned and humiliated.

CHAPTER FIFTEEN

OLE DEVIL'S TURKEY SHOOT

They had been arriving for the past few days, coming from the length and breadth of Texas, converging on the O.D. Connected house, gathering in for one purpose to enjoy the fun at Ole Devil's Turkey Shoot. Many of the visitors had travelled for a week or more. Some owned their own ranches, some prosperous businesses. There were cow-hands, soldiers, lawmen, possibly a few outlaws for Ole Devil held open house and all were welcome.

The welcome extended to the Lazy J, delivered along with the ranch's cattle found in the O.D. Connected and Double B's fall round-up. All the dudes were invited and from reports gathered from people who attended other Turkey Shoots, the visitors intended to come along.

Word of their coming brought an air of expectancy to the O.D. Connected ranch hands. They looked forward to dude women to augment the numbers at the dance in the evening. This in turn would reduce the number of men required to wear heifer brand, being marked with a piece of white rag around the arm, acting as ladies in the dance sets and carrying with it the dubious privilege of sitting among the womenfolk during the intervals.

On the porch of the main house Ole Devil Hardin sat greeting the new arrivals. It had long been the established convention that on arrival the visitors would come up and greet Ole Devil before settling in to the business of enjoying the event to the full. He watched the arrival of the Clements brothers, a hard-case bunch but kin for all of that. On greeting Ole Devil the eldest brother, Manning, announced his intention of showing Mark Counter the finer points of the art of wrestling. He tried every year, but never suc-ceeded. Ole Devil gave his permission and Manning de-parted to ask Hondo Fog to act as judge.

Next group to arrive were the dudes from the Lazy J. They came, for the most part, in the comfortably fitted wagons from the spread. Drinkwater brought Defluer and Paulette in a buggy and Marie Rambeau travelled the same way, driving herself in a fast buggy which might be needed to get her away if things went wrong.

At the corral a party of cowhands under Waco's command unhitched the teams and put the horses up for their guests. Marie saw the way some of the cowhands eyed her up and down. It gave her a sense of eagerness, an assurance that she would have but little trouble in stirring up a whole mess of trouble. However, before any of the corral party could say anything she saw Buck Blaze bearing down on her, at least from his smile of welcome she assumed it was Buck. In this case her guess proved to be correct and he led her off. She did not see that her horse was unhitched from the buggy, placed in the corral and the buggy itself stood in line out of the way of other arrivals.

'Did you catch your bear?' she asked.

'Why sure. He ran for near on five hours, but we caught him. I'll let you have his hide if you like.'

'Thank you kindly,' she answered. 'Where are we going?'

'You'll have to meet Uncle Devil, then I'll collect my rifle and we'll head on out to win us a turkey.'

Knowing what would be expected Bill Acre, who came on his horse and with the Drinkwater party, led the others towards the main house. They had seen Marie meet Buck Blaze and Drinkwater felt his scheme might start working this afternoon.

'Which is Dusty Fog?' Defluer asked.

'I'll point him out,' Acre replied, then he nodded ahead to where a small, insignificant looking cowhand stood talking with a handsome blond giant. 'That's him.'

'The tall man?' asked Defluer, noting the spread of the blond giant's shoulders. His witnesses might have been wrong about the colour of the hair.

'Nope, that's Mark Counter. I mean the other one.'

At that moment Dusty swung from Mark and walked to greet the new arrivals. Drinkwater studied Dusty, seeing beyond a small man, seeing the quiet assurance, the air of command, the bearing of a born leader. And yet Dusty Fog, without his high-heeled boots, would be half an inch smaller than Drinkwater.

'Howdy,' Dusty greeted. 'Make yourself to home. The shooting's down that way, it only costs a dollar to enter and if you don't have your own rifle one of the boys'll likely loan you one.'

'Thank you,' Drinkwater replied. 'I'm Drinkwater, from the Lazy J. This is Aristes Defluer and his daughter, Paulette.'

'My pleasure. I'm Dusty Fog.'

He turned and left them after a few moments of conversation for he had much to do in the matter of seeing the Turkey Shoot was enjoyed by all. Defluer watched Dusty fade into the crowd and wondered if he could be the same Captain Fog who led Troop 'C' Texas Light Cavalry in the war and whose name had often been in the Northern newspapers. The man who, if the ex-soldier's story be true, shot Defluer's son in the back. Yet he was no burly black bearded giant. He seemed a pleasant, if remarkably efficient young man. Defluer swore he would get to the bottom of the mystery before he left the O.D. Connected that day.

Dusty passed Johnny Raybold and Betty Hardin. It came as something of a surprise to see Betty out here instead of attending to the woman's work which must be done. Nor could Dusty ever remember seeing Johnny look so all-fired out and out scared as he did right now.

'What's wrong?' he asked.

'Nothing!' Betty replied, just too quickly.

'Nothing, huh?' Dusty drawled, then he grinned at Johnny. 'Uncle Devil's on the porch. Go up and ask him, Johnny. I reckon you'll be some surprised at the way he acts.'

'Which same's what's worrying me,' answered Johnny.

Only he didn't say it to Dusty for the small Texan walked away. Betty gave an angry gasp, then started to smile.

'That cousin of mine get's smarter every day. I sure didn't think it showed.'

Johnny nodded. He squared back his shoulders, set his jaw determinedly and headed for the porch. He saw Ole Devil just finish speaking with some dudes and went forward. Ole Devil watched him, frosty eyes seeming to dig down into his soul. Johnny felt like heading for the corral and taking off for the tall timber. He saw Charlie Goodnight, master cowman, first trail boss and man who learned the early lessons and made the inter-State drives north possible. Goodnight came from where he had been sitting and Johnny felt like a man reprieved from hanging. Only it did not last for Goodnight caught Ole Devil's wink and fell back again.

Stepping on to the porch Johnny took a deep breath. The die was cast, he could not back down. Nor could he seem to get his usually glib tongue working.

'Er—I—that is——!'

'Look, boy,' Ole Devil said gently. 'If you're aiming to ask if you can marry Betty the answer's yes.'

If Ole Devil had upped and hit Johnny in the face with a sock full of bull-droppings the young cowhand couldn't have been more surprised. Sure he had been seeing more than a little of Betty, but he couldn't ever recollect ever giving the others any sign of how he felt about her. So Johnny stood there with his mouth hanging open and for once words failed him.

'Way you're acting you'd think I was senile,' Ole Devil went on. 'I've seen it coming for days now. Can we announce the engagement tonight at the dance?'

'If you would, sir.'

'Tommy!' Ole Devil barked. 'Bring the burgundy and three glasses. Sit down, John, I want to hear something about you.'

Betty had stood awaiting an explosion, not sure how her grandfather would react when he heard the news. She knew everything was all right when she saw Tommy Okasi bring out the burgundy. With a smile Betty turned and headed towards the cook-shack to lend a hand with the refreshments.

Meantime things were going well, very well for Marie Rambeau. Half an hour after the exhibition wrestling match she looked like she had got things going her way. Two cowhands, one from the O.D. Connected and the other riding for Double B, stood facing each other, faces hot and angry.

'Whyn't you smoke off?' one asked. 'The lady was with me.'

'Like hell she was,' replied the other. 'You Double B

146

bunch are all the same and the lady wanted me along with her.'

'What's coming off here?'

The words came in a soft gentle drawl. But they separated the two men, brought about a sudden end to hostilities. She swung around to find the small, insignificant cowhand walking towards her group. Still not remembering who Dusty was she wondered how he came to exert such authority over the other men.

'The lady wanted me to show her around, Dusty,' replied the O.D. Connected hand.

'She asked me first!' objected the Double B rider.

'You want me to settle this for you?' asked Dusty.

'Why sure,' agreed the Double B hand, knowing Dusty would be completely fair and impartial.

'Be best,' agreed the O.D. Connected rider.

'Easy enough done. Two into one won't go. Likewise there's plenty of young ladies back that ways. You pair head off and find them. I'll take care of the lady.'

The O.D. Connected hand grinned. 'I never argues with the boss.'

'Nor me, let's go look for some pretty little gals.'

Marie could have screamed in rage and frustration. Her efforts had been stopped again. Irrationally she laid the full blame for it all on Dusty's head. Then for the first time she realised who he must be.

'You're Captain Dusty Fog, aren't you?' she asked.

'That's right enough, ma'am. I've some advice for you. Don't try and stir up any more fights among the boys.'

She glared at him, trying to look innocent and enraged at the suggestion. 'I don't know what you mean!'

'No, ma'am?' Dusty drawled. 'Between Buck and the Ysabel Kid for a start. And Manning Clements told me about your little try with him. Now these two fool kids. You may have the idea it'd be fun to have men fight over you, could be for all I know. But not here, ma'am, not here. We've never had any trouble at a Turkey Shoot and we don't aim to have it spoiled now.'

For a long moment they looked at each other without a word. Suddenly Marie became aware that mere inches did not make a man. She knew that strong willed as Buck had been here stood the strongest of them all. Dusty Fog was the power here, the man she must destroy before she could hope to succeed in her plan. She knew it would not be easy. Perhaps it might be better to throw the job over, extract such money as she could from Drinkwater and go east.

'I apologise,' she said, sounding humble. 'I will cause no more trouble for your friends.'

'No, ma'am, it wouldn't be wise,' Dusty replied. 'Enjoy yourself, ma'am.'

They went in opposite directions. Marie turned the corner of the house and bumped into a tall, slim and very handsome man. She had been so absorbed that she did not recognise him at first, seeing only a rather dandified gambler's clothes and a silver topped cane.

'I came as quickly as I could, Marie cherie.'

She looked up and recognition came to her. This was the answer to the telegraph message she sent in Diggers Wells. The man before her looked handsome, yet there was a hint of real cruelty behind the smiling mask and Marie knew Vincent de Sarde had a heart as cold as her own.

'I'm pleased to see you, Vincent,' she replied.

'You didn't bring me all this way just to tell me that?'

'Of course not. There is money to be made here, big money.'

'Not by gambling?' he asked, still smiling.

'No, by killing at least one man.'

For all the change showing in de Sarde's face Marie might have asked him to take a drink of coffee. He watched the girl's face, seeing, not that he ever doubted it, that she was in deadly earnest.

'Who?' he asked.

'I'd better tell you the full story first, then you will see how best we can turn it to our advantage,' Marie answered. 'Let's walk around so that we are not so noticeable. I have been hired to stir up trouble among the men here.'

'And you need help to do *that*,' de Sarde answered, taking her arm and walking towards where a horse race was about to start. 'Among a bunch of country clodhoppers like these bumpkins?'

'They happen to be remarkably intelligent bumpkins,' she admitted. 'One in particular. Dusty Fog, he is the second-in-command of the ranch here and the other men follow him as if he were some kind of god. While he lives I

148

might as well be an old hag for all the notice the others take of me. He must die.'

'It might be better if he did die,' agreed de Sarde, 'then we have a hold over the people who hired you. Unless they pay well we inform the Rio Hondo men of their activities, from a safe distance, and let the cards fall where they will.'

'I hadn't thought of that,' she said seriously. 'Drinkwater wouldn't want his part in this known.'

They stood watching the horse race for a moment. All around them people cheered and yelled their delight. Marie felt bored with the business and looked at de Sarde.

'How will you kill him?'

'A duel is out. It is hard to arrange things so the other side looks the aggressor and leaves me with the choice of weapons. Even if I did, the chance of these chaw-bacons owning a set of duelling swords is not very likely and I do not intend facing Dusty Fog with a pistol in my hand. Yes, my petite angel, I have heard of him.'

'Then why not tonight?' she replied. 'I will try and get him outside. You can wait in the darkness and as he passes——'

De Sarde smiled, and twisted the knob of his walking cane between his hands. 'A single thrust and none will know who killed him. Dusty Fog will not see the light of dawn tomorrow, Marie, my love.'

CHAPTER SIXTEEN

STEEL IN THE NIGHT

Lights hung suspended from ropes which stretched between the main house, the bunkhouse, the cook-shack and the big building known as the hall and in which the Turkey Shoot ball would take place. After dark everybody, the men from their various occupations, the women, all of them, including the visitors to the Lazy J, from the work of cleaning up after a meal, made for the hall. They were drawn in by the music which already welled up inside.

For such an important occasion cowhand clothes would definitely not do for the members of the floating outfit. So, not without protest on the part of the Ysabel Kid, they donned their best; cutaway coats, frilly fronted shirts with black string ties, town style trousers and shiny shoes. Mark Counter looked even more distinguished than usual in this outfit. Dusty wore a grey coat and for once looked slightly less significant and more of what he really was.

One person who showed some interest in the arrival of Dusty and the others was Marie Rambeau. After their first meeting she and de Sarde stayed away from each other and the man had not entered the hall. He wanted to stay outside so that none might miss him and inquire into his absence when Dusty Fog's body was found. She glanced at Dusty and passed from the room, going out towards the ladies' back-house. This lay out beyond the forge and from the shadows of the forge stepped de Sarde, leading her out of sight.

'Well?' he asked.

'You can't miss him, he's wearing a grey cutaway coat.'

'Good, can you get him out here later, once the dance is really going well?'

'I can. I'll send him along at about ten o'clock. And I'll meet you by the corral, I'm leaving with you.'

'All right. I'll finish him, hide his body in here. By the time they find it we'll be well clear, even riding double. Have you a gun?'

She hefted the vanity bag. 'A Derringer,' she replied.

'Keep it, you may need it. Now go back and stay away from here. I'll see you by the corral at five minutes past ten. I'll go down and make sure my horse is ready to leave.'

Marie turned and walked away. The stage was set, now all she had to do would be wait, keep an eye on the time and at ten o'clock send Dusty Fog out to meet his death.

Never one to dance much Dusty Fog walked around the edge of the floor, making small talk, greeting friends, hearing news of mutual acquaintances. He had a talk with Drinkwater, discussing the cattle business and the idea of a ranch on which rich dudes could spend a holiday. He made suggestions which Drinkwater mentally noted as having possibilities, not the least was the hiring of a pack of good hounds to supply his guests with a chance to hunt down and shoot a cougar or bear.

They looked much alike in height and in dress style, a thing Marie Rambeau had not noticed, or if noticing had thought nothing about. De Sarde had seen both of them during the dark, but then Dusty wore his range clothes and Drinkwater, on Bill Acre's advice, left his coat in the buggy for the events of the day and collected it after the meal, to wear inside the hall.

Seeing Drinkwater and Dusty talking, Defluer decided to try to learn the truth about his son's death. So he crossed the room and joined the conversation. After mentioning various items of interest, Defluer swung the talk to firearms and the war.

'Did you ever meet up with any Lancers, Captain Fog?' Defluer inquired.

'Only once,' Dusty replied. 'We were on patrol and jumped them.'

'Did they fight well?'

'Nope,' Dusty replied, wishing the subject was over.

'They didn't?' Defluer asked.

'They were badly led,' Dusty explained. 'Only one officer showed any sign of sense, a captain he was, as far as I can remember. At least, he was the only officer who tried to rally the men. One of the other officers shot him in the back, trying to cut loose at us. If that hadn't happened, he might have made things hot; us only being a company to their battalion. The rest scattered, he was the only officer shot.'

Defluer sucked in a deep breath, but controlled his emotions with commendable skill. There was no reason why Dusty should lie, or fabricate such a story. The small Texan did not know Defluer's connection with the dead captain. All too clearly the financier saw what had happened. Eager to make money, the man found by Pinkertons had told a pack of lies. So Defluer had nursed a hatred against an innocent man for years. More than that, the same man had just painted Aristes in glowing colours. Praise of that kind from Captain Fog was indeed praise of a high order.

More of the guests drifted over to join Dusty and meet the Eastern men. The subject turned to cattle and Dusty attached little importance to Defluer's earlier questioning. Inside ten minutes the conversation had almost passed from his mind and the festivities continued.

About an hour later Basil Drinkwater felt the need to relieve himself. He turned on his heel and left Bill Acre by the punch bowl. He walked out into the night, turning to one side and passing around the corner of the hall, heading for the men's back-house which lay to the far side of the blacksmith's forge.

He thought of seeing Marie Rambeau and finding out what progress, if any, she might have made. Yet if she had stirred up trouble it did not show, nor had he seen any sign of it all day. Somehow it no longer mattered to him. An instinct, born of years in big business, warned him when to call a thing quits. He knew he could never split the close bonds of the Rio Hondo clan, nor could he take over their lands.

The Lazy J paid well, gave a good return for its cost of upkeep and would pay better when he put Captain Fog's ideas into practice. His Uvalde holdings were safe enough and would pay for themselves. So he decided to pay off Marie Rambeau and forget the Rio Hondo.

With that thought in mind he passed alongside the blacksmith's forge, his light grey cutaway jacket showing up well in the darkness.

Marie Rambeau came to Dusty Fog's side, her face showing worry, concern and nervous anxiety.

'The two youngsters you stopped earlier!' she gasped. 'They started arguing with each other and went out behind the forge to settle it.'

'So?'

'One of them has a gun! I saw it under his coat. And they've both been drinking. I'm afraid of what might——'

'You ought to have thought of that sooner,' Dusty replied.

His words carried to Betty Hardin as the girl passed among the crowd. Betty watched Marie Rambeau, seeing the worried expression fade as Dusty turned and left the room. Marie turned and made for the side door, collecting her vanity bag as she went by and Betty followed on her heels. The woman was up to something and Betty aimed to see what happened. At the same time, shortly after Dusty, Bill Acre also left the room.

Vincent de Sarde watched the man in the grey coat coming towards the forge. Slowly, so as to make no sound, he drew the thin steel blade from inside its cane sheath. The man would be passing to the far side, making for the men's back-house. Yet he was small and wore a grey coat, he looked like Dusty Fog's height, there was not likely to be another man wearing the same style clothes come by, especially so near ten o'clock.

The man passed. De Sarde stepped out and lunged. He shot out the sword-stick blade in a masterly thrust, sinking it home in just the right spot. He saw the small man's back arch, heard the muffled gasp of pain, felt his victim going down and sliding from his sword blade. It was over, he had done his part, now he must hide the body and get clear.

'What the——!' a voice began from behind him.

De Sarde whirled around, the sword still red with human blood. Out in the open stood a small man, a man in a grey cutaway coat, a man with dusty blond hair showing in the moon's waning light.

'You!' de Sarde hissed. 'Then who——'

He saw the small man move forward, empty handed yet menacing. Out into the half light sprang de Sarde, his sword driving forward a thrust. To one side, by the women's back-house, he heard a scream, and knew he had been seen. He knew his proposed ambush place was badly selected, learned it too late, people were coming and going all the time and the female back-house had been in use even as he came out to kill. The woman must have come out and seen him. Her screams would bring people on the run. He must kill Dusty Fog and make good his escape, or he would never have the chance.

So de Sarde lunged into an attack. He thought he struck at a gun-fighter who had no idea what a duelling sword was for. In this he made a grave error. Inside the house hung duelling swords and Dusty Fog learned to handle a blade almost as soon as he could walk.

At the last instant Dusty weaved aside. A hand which could draw and shoot a Colt in less than half a second stabbed out. Fingers like iron clamps closed on de Sarde's wrist, strength which took him completely by surprise heaved him forward and off balance.

Dusty's free hand lashed around, fingers extended, thumb bent over palm, edge cutting in under de Sarde's chin and full into his throat. The killer's gasped-out curse died in a strangled croak as the deadly *tegatana*, the hand-sword of karate, lashed home. Pain welled through him. He could not breathe. The sword fell from his hand. Dusty released his hold and chopped again, his hand scything into the side of de Sarde's throat and dropping him like a backbroke rabbit.

Feet thudded behind Dusty. Hondo Fog, Mark, Waco and the Kid arrived, coming to investigate the screams. Bill Acre was not with them. He saw his boss go down and Dusty's intervention, then he headed for the other side of the building.

'What happened, Dusty?' Hondo asked.

'I don't know. Just came on to them after this fancy dressed *hombre* killed the other one. You'd best ask him.'

Kneeling by de Sarde's twitching, purple-faced body Mark looked up. 'Happen we don't get a doctor here *pronto*,' he said quietly, 'this *hombre*'ll never tell us.'

'This one'll never talk again,' put in the Kid. 'It's the boss of the Lazy J. He's dead.'

Hondo threw a glance towards the hall, hearing the music and knowing the band and the womenfolk would keep everybody's attention off the outside. He looked to where a white-faced dude woman came towards them.

'Take her to the house, Waco,' he ordered. 'I'll send a woman along as soon as I can.'

At the other side of the building Marie Rambeau ran towards the corral and the saddled horse. She had heard the screams and knew she must get away quickly. If de Sarde had not arrived before her she would take the horse and ride out. Her skill on a horse would carry her clear and she had a trail to follow which would finally take her to the Lazy J where she could force more money from Drinkwater and get far away from Texas.

She might have to throw de Sarde to the wolves, but doubted if he would be taken alive. She had wired him to help her out, brought him to the Rio Hondo, but she felt no shred of conscience trouble at leaving him. The horse was ahead of her and she knew de Sarde would desert her with as little worry had he been given the chance.

'Hold it, girlie!'

Marie heard the rustle of a dress and turned to face Betty Hardin. Her hand went into the mouth of the vanity bag and closed on the butt of the Remington Double Derringer.

'Keep back!' she hissed.

'Take your hand out,' Betty replied. 'If you don't I'll stuff it and the bag down your throat.'

She could do it too, even though Marie stood a head taller and weighed heavier. Only to do it Marie would have to be close enough to reach. Betty didn't think the other woman reached inside her bag to find a powder puff. Getting close enough to put Tommy Okasi's training into practice would likely cost her a bullet in the stomach.

Marie's hand lifted from the bag, holding the snub nosed Derringer. She knew she could never mount the horse while Betty Hardin stood watching. So, the way Marie saw it, there was only one thing to do. Her finger started to tighten on the trigger.

A shot roared in the darkness, from behind Betty. Marie Rambeau stiffened. Her face still looked the same, only now there was a blue rimmed hole just above her eyes. Then she fell in a limp, crumpled heap.

Never had Betty been so close to death before. She stared at the other woman, at the Derringer lying by a limp hand. It took all Betty's strength of will to hold control of herself.

155

She turned to see who had saved her life.

'She set the boss up for a kill, with that killer she brought in,' Bill Acre said grimly as he came forward, his Merwin and Hulbert Pocket Army revolver in his hand. 'I was too late to cut in and Cap'n Fog handled the other one. So I came after her. Take it kind if you'd not start yelling, or say which way I went.'

'There's no need to run,' Betty replied gently, stepping to his side and laying a hand on his arm. 'Do you think anybody in the Rio Hondo will hurt you for saving my life?' They stood facing each other. Inside the hall Jimmo yelled that the shot was no more than some fool cowhand trying to have a joke. The music went on and the people carried on with their dancing, talking, drinking. Hondo Fog appeared for a moment and disappeared again with his wife but the crowd thought nothing of it.

Down by the corral the Kid and Mark Counter arrived fast. They saw the dead woman, and Betty standing by Bill Acre's side.

'Are you all right, Betty?' Mark asked.

'Yes. This gent saved my life,' Betty replied. She did not look at the body but waved a hand towards it. 'Take her—the body, down the back of the house.'

'Sure,' replied Mark. 'And thanks, mister, this little gal means a lot to us.'

Acre holstered the weapon. 'I'll tote the body for you. Show me where to take it.'

'I'll do that,' drawled the Kid. 'Mark, you get Betty back to the hall and take care of the folks.'

Not one of the guests knew of the happenings beyond the hall's walls. Jimmo and the band kept playing and Hondo Fog returned, his face showing nothing of his thoughts. He crossed the floor to Ole Devil's group and dropped his voice.

'You best come along with us, Devil, and you, Uncle Mannen. Reckon you had as well, Mr. Defluer. Only don't make a fuss, your partner's met with an accident.'

Defluer threw a look to where Paulette stood laughing and talking with Sue and Red Blaze. He followed the other men across the room and on the bandstand the ranch cook began another dance set.

'What happened, honey?' Johnny Raybold asked Betty.

'There was a killing,' she replied. 'Don't talk about it, Johnny. Please.'

The men gathered in Ole Devil's gun-decorated study. Ole Devil sat his wheelchair in the centre, Judge Mannen Blaze at his left side. Hondo Fog stood by Bill Acre and the floating outfit ringing the room. Defluer sank into a chair, face ashy and pale. His eyes went from face to face, they were tall men, tough, hard men, but the tallest to his eyes was the small, dusty blond haired young man who stood at Ole Devil's right hand, the man called Dusty Fog.

'You'd better start from the beginning, sir,' Dusty said to Defluer and none of the others questioned his right to open the debate.

'How can I tell Paulette?' Defluer replied, his voice hoarse and tired. 'She loved Basil Drinkwater and in his way he loved her. Or came as near to loving her as he could to anything.'

'Why'd he bring de Sarde in?' asked Hondo.

'The boss didn't!' Acre growled. 'It was that hellcat I killed. She brought him in here when she couldn't stir up fuss between you Rio Hondo boys.'

'Let me explain, Bill,' Defluer put in. 'Although basically Bill has told you why Rambeau was here.'

Slowly, then firmly as he got his words coming out, Defluer told of the plan to take over the Rio Hondo. He held nothing back, not even his own part in it, or the part he might have played in it. The other men listened without speaking, hearing him out.

'You knew Johnny Raybold was being set up for a kill?' Dusty asked quietly.

'I take full responsibility for knowing, Captain Fog.'

'Why'd you tie into this thing in the first place?' Dusty went on. 'Because your son died in the war, because you thought we killed him?'

'Something like that. I heard a story, it blamed a man I thought to be you for shooting my son in the back. I know now I was wrong. That was one motive for my joining with Basil.'

'How about you, Acre?' Hondo put in.

'Bill tried to talk Basil out of the idea,' Defluer spoke up before the other man could say a word.

'He was set on it,' Acre went on. 'I told him he couldn't

157

take over the Rio Hondo, told him that girl couldn't break your clan up.'

'You stood by him!' said the Ysabel Kid, sounding Comanche mean.

'I took his pay. I threw my bedroll in his outfit's wagon,' replied Acre. 'If I could have stopped him I would. If not I aimed to stand by and try to get him clear before it got too late.'

Once more silence dropped on the room. At last Defluer looked up at the faces before him.

'What do you intend to do?'

'Try the killer for murder,' Hondo replied. 'If he lives, the doctor's having trouble keeping his windpipe open.'

'And me?'

'Nothing,' Hondo answered. 'You lost a good friend. It cost us nothing. We reckon you've paid enough.'

A knock came at the door and Tommy Okasi entered carrying a buff coloured telegraph message. He held it to Defluer. The man opened the envelope and looked down at the printed words. His face lost its colour for the words spelled out a message he had been afraid might come.

'Bad news?' Ole Devil asked.

'There has been a run on the Market. I've lost a considerable sum of money I might have saved had I not been in Texas.'

'It busted you clean?' Hondo asked.

'Not quite. But it's taken a lot.'

'You can get some of it back,' Dusty drawled. 'Take over the Lazy J. Put Bill Acre in as segundo. You'll find it'll pay you well.'

'You'd let me after what's happened?'

'Never was a hand for kicking a man when he's down, none of us,' Ole Devil answered. 'You satisfied with everything, Mannen?'

'I reckon so,' replied Judge Mannen Blaze.

'You, Hondo?'

'If you are.'

'I am. And you, Dustine?'

'I'll go with you, sir,' Dusty replied. 'Which same we'd better go. It's near on midnight and I sure don't want to face Cousin Betty if you haven't announced her engagement tonight.'

THE END

Introducing Brady Anchor and Jefferson Trade in the latest exciting
J. T. EDSON:

TWO MILES TO THE BORDER

Who had taught Spit Merton to carry out a mighty slick, well-planned robbery?

Why did Merton and his gang take only fifty thousand dollars from the Rocksprings' bank when they could easily have emptied the safe?

What did the dying owlhoot mean when he said that his companions were 'Going to church, two miles to the border'?

Figuring that the answers might show sufficient profit to help keep them in a manner to which they had always been too poor to become accustomed, Brady Anchor and Jefferson Trade set out to try to learn them. If they had realised that their search for enlightenment would bring them into contact with Widow Snodgrass and her Daughters of the Lord, they would have been a heap less willing to set about it.

0 552 09113 8 – 25p

A SELECTED LIST OF FINE NOVELS
from the
CORGI WESTERN RANGE

All these books are available at your bookshop or newsagent: or can be ordered direct from the publisher. Just tick the titles you want and fill in the form below.

CORGI BOOKS, Cash Sales Department, P.O. Box 11, Falmouth, Cornwall.
Please send cheque or postal order. No currency, and allow 6p per book to cover the cost of postage and packing in the U.K., and overseas.

NAME ....

ADDRESS ....

(JULY 72) ....